I hope t/
gets you c
for the beauty ?
of the river as I

Love Mike

2007
Dec.

SIDE CANYONS

SIDE CANYONS

Laurie Wagner Buyer

Five Star • Waterville, Maine

Copyright © 2004 by Laurie Wagner Buyer

First Edition, Second Printing

Set in 11 pt. Plantin by Ramona Watson.

Printed in the United States on permanent paper.

Library of Congress Cataloging-in-Publication Data

Buyer, Laurie Wagner, 1954–
    Side canyons / by Laurie Wagner Buyer.—1st ed.
      p. cm.
    ISBN 1-59414-115-0 (hc : alk. paper)
    1. Colorado River (Colo.-Mexico)—Fiction.   2. Grand Canyon (Ariz.)—Fiction.   3. Women adventurers—Fiction. I. Title.
PS3552.U8944S53 2004
  813'.54—dc22   2003065574

For the River

On the Ranch

Without Angie there wouldn't be a story.

Well, there'd be a story, but not this one and it wouldn't have taken place on the Colorado River in the Grand Canyon. Years ago along the banks of another wild river, I met Angie at a rustic cabin tucked between Glacier National Park and Flathead National Forest. Months before, she had been the woman sleeping in the upstairs bedroom with the bearded, buckskinned man who was now my lover. Two years older, but not much wiser, I felt tentative and shy when pixie-cute, still-in-her-teens Angie appeared on our snow-covered, flagstone doorstep to meet the woman who had taken her place. Affectionate, endearing Angie. We loved each other from the moment of our first hug and when she left at the end of a week of constant chatter and laughter, we wrote often, me telling tales of work-worn days, she sharing stories of college life. Then, Angie disappeared.

In 1998, two decades after her last letter, I heard from Angie again. She had traveled back to Montana to see the old homestead and mutual friends gave her my address. With an abode in the East, and a master's degree in environmental sciences, Angie worked as a toxic waste consultant and an illustrator. I had turned into a ranch wife and poet, settling on the South Fork of the South Platte River in Colorado, not far from Angie's childhood haunts. Angie visited me on the ranch. Then, I visited her at her family's summer place.

At Wellington Lake

On a point of rocks we stop to stare
across calm water, two women,
who, after twenty years of silence,
have discovered each other again.

Her delicate flesh still hangs on
bird bones and she is airy as ever,
moving light like restless wings,
her eyes the color of September trees.

Bareheaded, her short cropped mane,
beginning to strand with silver,
bounces against the graceful arc
of her neck when she turns to speak.

At eighteen, a runaway from boarding
school, she lived for a few fall months
with the same man I would later love
and then leave after eight angry years.

"He never loved me," she confesses.
"Nor me!" I answer. The following
quiet is solemn until we begin to laugh
like the Montana loons we remember.

The sun sinks behind stone spires
and we retrace our steps, stopping

in the shelter of thick trees to squat
and pee, listening to dusk speak:

wind rustling the last aspen leaves,
a rill whispering over rocks,
squirrels scurrying into the highest
branches of a battered ponderosa pine.

We walk on, chatting as sisters do,
the conversation meandering down
different paths, to work and art,
families, our current men,

but, then, we find ourselves
drifting back, like loose horses to
familiar stalls, to the man who first
brought us, somewhat hesitant, together.

The night folds around us, a worn quilt
made of darkness and stars, as we sit
in her great-grandfather's cabin eating
minestrone soup and homemade bread.

The warmth of the wood stove encourages
us to stay up late, our talk interrupted only
by an owl's eerie cry, and an unexpected
visit from a red fox courting bread crusts.

Curled in sleeping bags under the eaves,
we whisper in the unlit room, our words
returning to the strange soul who now sleeps
alone, who writes long letters to us both.

Some women say a mother's love is the most enduring.
But, childless, I disagree. The most lasting
love to be found is that between two women
who have loved, and then left, the same man.

Angie and I continued to correspond. Sometimes I re-hashed our past, trying to make sense of the way one man's violent anger had scarred my life. As close as we were, I didn't know how to tell Angie about the shame I harbored because I had gone on living with a person who practiced random acts of cruelty, the constant demeaning criticism, the small, hard slaps meant to keep me in line. How could I tell her what it felt like to hide inside myself to be safe, how fear forced me to seek silence as a shelter? And, how at times, when I could no longer bear the abuse, the injustice of name-calling and put-downs, I erupted, the temper I'd inherited from my father throwing gas on the flames of our altercations.

Though I found no forgiveness for myself, I fought hard to forgive him, to make excuses for the erratic behavior that mirrored my father's. I called his psychotic outbursts ar-tistic tantrums. Excused his pistol-brandishing tirades against the government because he'd been in Vietnam. While not wanting to condone his vulgar misogyny, I never protested it either. I merely shrank from the cynicism that bordered on hatred because he had a complicated relation-ship with his mother. When he raged his discontent with the whole world, I learned to stay small, to shut up, because to speak out, to disagree, meant being clobbered.

But, more often than not, I quit trying to exhume and examine the unpalatable past. I kept my diatribes to Angie riveted on challenges like how to keep my husband happy and ways to freelance my way to financial independence. Most of all, I worried the philosophical problem of why love never seemed to be enough to keep things in balance.

Disfigured

The taste of old blood churns in my stomach
telling my mouth it's done more than minor battle.

Fingers feel each inch of psychological skin.
Where isn't it bruised? Where doesn't it hurt?

Kneeling in front of the toilet, choking,
saliva and bile rise in uneasy sickening waves.

I massage my heart and liver, pray for healing,
begging my body not to vomit itself into oblivion.

I wake wearing two pairs of pants, two turtlenecks,
two pairs of socks, a sweatshirt under a terrycloth robe.

Is this protective armor? Is this enough to block the
    blows
that still surface after all these patient years of
    forgiving?

You never meant to hurt me, but in your blind
    striking out
I was in your way, trying to hold you, comfort you.

Bruises fade and disappear. Wounds heal. Even scar
    tissue
stretches and softens. Even so, I see myself, disfigured.

When Angie invited me to go on a river trip with her and three other women, I fussed, arguing that I had no money, no time, no energy, and I was working on an MFA. No matter how many tests they ran, doctors could not diagnose my constant fatigue, headaches, joint pain, and digestion problems.

"Angie," I told her, "I'm running on empty. Besides, I'm afraid John won't like this. He hates it when I'm gone."

"What's he going to do, divorce you?" she joked.

"No, but when he disapproves, when he's hurt, he gives me the cold-shoulder-I'm-not-talking-to-you treatment. The deliberate shunning goes on for days. He makes me feel like I'm a horrible wife," I said.

"You know better than that, Laurie. He'll pout for awhile, but he'll get over it," she said.

"Maybe, but aside from not wanting to face the fallout, there isn't any money. Angie, things are so bad with the cattle market that John's talking about selling out again," I said.

"Laurie, I'll loan you the money. You can take the rest of your life to pay me back. Please, please, please come with me. Just send in two hundred dollars for your reservation and you'll have a whole year to think about it."

An inner voice, echoing Angie's, urged me to go. I acquiesced and sent in my check, but I kept the river trip a secret. If John didn't know what I had planned, then he couldn't accuse me of deserting him. Weary, too sick to be serious about an adventure anyway, I slipped the file labeled Grand Canyon into the back of a drawer, and pushed any thoughts of the river into the back of my mind.

Six months later I still wasn't thinking about the river. I thought only about the pain that kept me stuck in bed for days, and the fact that I could no longer help John with the outdoor chores. Mired in the mud of eight years of counseling, past the point of senseless tears, tired of warding off ridiculous thoughts of self-destruction, I turned to holistic healing for answers.

Live Analysis

Clear black plasma hosts
a swarm of round red cells,
some, misshaped into tear drops,
bear the burden of protein linkage.

In this alive dark-as-night sky,
the nebulae of white cells,
packed with frenetic energy,
pick off small stars of bacteria.

Here and there, misty patches
mark where worn-out white cells
stopped working and left behind
angel-shaped, vaporous shells.

One little prick, one tiny drop,
and all that I am is micro-visible,
beautiful and beguiling,
until my blood dies.

With treatment some of my strength returned, but a restive discontent plagued me. I returned from a spring morning walk and wrote in my journal: "This restlessness reminds me of the lone bluebird that appeared on a bristlecone branch, its flashing dash of color something between sapphire and sky, high up where the wind polishes ridge rocks of snow in mid-March before the sun swings farther south succoring enough warmth to melt groaning ice from the uterine lake. A single goose gropes the frozen edge with black-paddled feet, pacing round and round a patch of water that reflects a scrap of cloud and blue bareness in cinereous depths. Her plaintive cries carry out over an otherwise empty morning, sounding like the eye of spring opening. A cow elk grazes alone on a south slope hill, her rump burnished like ivory, her mane dark as a burnt biscuit. Countless herds pasture in the high country, but she stays apart in a place where twisted aspen push gnarly branches to the east and no leaves rustle in an uneasy breeze that gusts and sighs from snow-clotted ravines."

Angie e-mailed me: "You're going, aren't you, Laurie? Please come. It won't be the same without you."

I argued with her, argued with myself. Apprehension crawled around the edges of my outlook. An unidentifiable fear stalked my thoughts. I confided in Angie. I talked with others who'd been in the Canyon. They all said, "The river will change your life. You'll never regret going." Older adventurers, close friends, encouraged me, said "you must go" and sent me the money to pay expenses.

Irresolute, nervous about starting a fight, I didn't know how to tell John what I was thinking of doing. I scribbled in my journal: "chasing tail, tail chasing, what I fear most pursues me what I want most eludes me what I fear most pursues me what I want most eludes me what I fear most pursues me what I want most eludes me."

Besides, I didn't want my safe, well-accustomed life to change.

In late summer, Angie e-mailed me one last time: "Laurie, if you're not going to go, I know a gal who would jump at the chance to take your place."

I read through my brochures from Anasazi Expeditions, threw them in the trash. Then dug them out again. Piqued by the stupid struggle, I dashed off a check to pay for the trip, drove to town and put it in the mail before I changed my mind. I couldn't stand the image of myself at eighty mumbling, "Why didn't I go to the Canyon when I had the opportunity."

Angie called: "Did you tell John yet?"

"No," I said, "I don't want to make any waves right now."

"Laurie, you have to tell him. Do it. Now. It's unfair not to let him know."

John and I rode that afternoon, our horses making their slow way through dry sagebrush pastures to check cows and calves trailed down from Tumble Creek the week before. I tried several times to tell him, phrasing and rephrasing the words, but couldn't spit them out. They stuck in my throat like day-old breadcrumbs. Anxiety ate my attempts. I didn't want to ruin the idyllic day.

After supper, on the point of short-circuiting, I choked out, "John, I've been wrestling with a big decision for almost a year now."

"Now what?" he sighed, looking over the top of his reading glasses at me.

The sentence pushed past my lips in one long rush: "Angie invited me to go with her and three other women on a river trip through the Grand Canyon and I'm going."

"When?" he asked, setting aside his newspaper.

"In October," I answered.

"How long?" he asked.

"Less than two weeks," I answered.

"That's shipping season," he said.

"I know," I said. "Maybe you could hold the calves on the cows a little longer."

"Forget it. I can do it alone," he said, standing up.

"You could ask the neighbors to give you a hand," I suggested.

He just stared at me with unspoken reproach.

"Can I have a divorce?" he asked, beginning a game we'd played before.

"Sure," I said, trying to lighten the mood by being playful, "you go to town and get the papers and I'll sign them."

I knew I had him beat because he hated to go to town.

"You've been gone a lot," he said, staring out the window at Blue, the cow dog, harassing the log-perched cat. "First San Antonio for that writer's convention thing, then Vermont to school, now this?"

"I know," I said, trying not to push any wrong buttons.

"Why are you so unhappy?" he said.

"I'm not unhappy, John. I love it here. I'm just, well, restless, unfulfilled maybe, like I'm searching for something."

"Well, I wish I knew what the hell it is you're searching for," he said, walking out of the room.

"I don't know, John," I said to his retreating back, "maybe I'm searching for a part of me that was lost a long time ago."

Not knowing if his nonresponse meant that he had not heard me or that he chose to ignore me, I did not follow.

Weeping

All summer mucus membranes
seeped clear watery fluid
leaving me wet and annoyed
with a cloying "what now" feeling.

My healer said with sympathy:
No treatment. This is not infection,
but old irritation, inflammation,
(hot red inner eyes finally crying).
Leave it be. Let it grieve.

So when he knocked, polite,
handsome and erect, pressed
against my closed door,
for the first time in fifteen years
I could not let him in.

Go away, I gestured with a gentle move.
I'm mourning my slipped children,
my diseased womb cut out,
the accidents and abuse
of unforgotten lovers,
and my passion for you
past its peak and fading.

The decision made, I rushed around, turning frantic loops talking to travel agents, trying to organize what I needed to take, packing and unpacking a too-big duffle bag. Trepidation tailed me like a snake's rattle. I e-mailed Angie: "What are Tevas? What's splash gear? Where can I find camp suds? We go to the bathroom where? What the hell is a 'groover'?"

Angie replied: "River sandals, waterproof jacket and pants, at the sporting goods store, it's a miniature port-a-potty about the size of a five-gallon bucket."

I wrote back: "You're kidding?"

"Nope," she said. "Think of it as an outhouse without the house attached."

Sensing my apprehension and aloneness, Angie put me in touch with her cousin, Lana, in Denver who was going with us into the Canyon.

"Sure," Lana said, "come here. Let's travel together. Don't forget to bring a day pack, a wide-brimmed hat, fleece jacket and a couple of carabiners."

"God," I asked, "what's a carabiner?"

Lana laughed. "A large, metal clip. Just ask," she said. "The sales guy will show you what it's for."

To my surprise, John bolstered my spirits by chauffeuring me to outdoor stores.

"Thank you," I said, when we stopped for a rare lunch in town. "You're being very sweet."

"I just want you to go and have a good time."

"Really?"

"Yes, I mean it. Just go. Get your head on straight. Figure out who you are. You're sure not the girl I married anymore," he said.

"I know that. Will you be all right without me?" I asked.

"No," he said, popping a lone french fry in his mouth

and chugging down the last of his Coke. "I'm afraid."

"Of what?" I asked, pushing aside the remains of my salad.

"That you'll leave me," he said.

"Oh, John, that's ridiculous," I said.

"Maggie left me," he said, referring to his first wife, "and she took the kids."

"John, that was twenty years ago. I have no intention of leaving you. I'll only be gone twelve days. I'm coming back," I said.

"Okay," he said, "if you say so."

"What makes you so mistrustful? After all we've been through together," I began, but he cut me off.

"Hell, you don't need me anymore. You've got your poetry, all your writer friends, the bright lights and—" he was saying when I interrupted him.

"That is so unfair," I interjected.

"Let's go," he said, picking up the bill. "I've got hay to stack."

Nine feet above the ground, putting the third tier of hay on the '37 Chevy flatbed, I positioned a bale John had thrown up to me, kneed it into place, and stepped backward into nothing but air, falling spread-eagle, my arms wide, my one thought focused on not landing on the sharp hay hook still clenched in my hand.

I hit the just-cut, stubble-spongy ground with a resounding oomph. Every bit of air whooshed out of my lungs. Horrible pain said, "You're dead."

Somewhere behind me John laughed, urging me "get up, get up, get up."

Outrage acted like smelling salts and I struggled to stand, suck in air, and slap away his offer of help. I stumbled to a bale in the field and sat down.

"Why," I wheezed to John, who stood in front of me arms slack at his sides, "in God's name are you laughing?"

"Because," he said, the edge of nervous laughter still in his voice, "I'm so glad you're alive. I couldn't believe you stepped off the back of the truck. Why did you do that?"

"I didn't do it on purpose," I said.

"You just walked backwards off the truck. What were you thinking? Were you trying to kill yourself?" he asked.

"John, I—" I said.

"Don't you know I couldn't live without you," he said.

Everything spun inside me like a whirlwind.

"I can't do this anymore," I wanted to say.

Instead I shoved a puny exhale out of my lungs and said, "Let's finish this load."

"Are you sure you're okay?" John asked.

"Sure, as soon as I can breathe again," I said.

The cowboy mentality of never letting anyone know when it hurts took over. Two aspirin, a hot bath, a good night's sleep, and I'd be just fine. No one likes a complainer. No one trusts a quitter. I had to prove to John that I was tough enough to do the work, strong enough to be part of his life, worthy enough to be loved.

As we trundled the load into the barn I fought my own instinct to be honest. Why couldn't I come right out and say, "I love you. I love the ranch. But I'm sick of this. I'm falling apart, body and heart. Why do we have to endure so much hard work, heartache, tears, worry, no money, no future, no fun, so little laughter, such paltry moments of joy in return for so much sacrifice?"

Even as I asked the question, I knew the answer. I stayed silent to keep my words from wounding him.

Trying to prepare for the rigors of the trip, I walked daily, training by trekking up and down the steep ridge east of the ranch. A six-mile hike with loaded backpack left me wrung out and quivering with exertion. John looked the other way, shaking his head, saying nothing.

We didn't talk about the river. As a matter of fact, we didn't say much at all, except for the polite offerings of long-married people: "Please pass the pepper." "Did you sleep well?" "Will you have enough hay for another winter?" "Did you see the cat try to catch the hummingbird?" "I put shoes on your horse." "Thank you."

The day before my departure showed up like an unexpected visitor. I noted its arrival, gave it a serious nod. Then, I drove to town in the evening to teach a writing class sponsored by the library.

The women students sensed my underlying frenetic energy and our discussion turned from poetic techniques to teasing girl talk: "How many men?" "Did you tell John?" "I heard wedding rings are forbidden." "Are you taking a bikini?" "How many days without a telephone?" "Everyone bathes together in the river?"

"I'm scared," I said, choking on the words.

"About what?"

How could I tell them about the woman inside of me who was clawing like a cat in a cardboard box trying to get free?

"About going away," I said.

Everyone gathered around me for a group hug.

"Just go," they said. "Have an adventure. Everything will be the same when you come back."

Portrait of a Woman in a Box

She dreams of chain saws, hatchets, chisels,
even of beaver with long sharp incisors.
She's been on her back so long
all she knows how to do is dream.
Long ago she wore away her fingernails,
clawing, wore out her knees, kicking.
Not the kind to scream she works
at being rational: It's warm here and dry,
soft underneath on the patchwork quilt
she hand-stitched out of emptiness,
and a chink near a knothole lets in air and light.
She's never idle. Cat-like she licks the wood
above her face, picks the splinters from her tongue
and saves them because someday
when she finally sands her way through,
they'll be the kindling she ignites with her eyes,
turning the funeral box into a personal pyre.

Driving home I researched the reason why the river frightened me. Ever since moving west I'd lived in the company of rivers and creeks: at the confluence of Colt's Creek with the Northfork of the Flathead River in Montana, on the banks of Eagle Creek on the IX Ranch, along Dickson Creek in the Bitterroot Mountains, at the juncture of Tosi and Tepee Creek near the Wind River Mountains, between Little Twin and Big Twin Creeks on the Upper Green River in Wyoming. I knew rivers. I knew water. Even though I'd never rafted a big river like the Colorado, I'd canoed on lakes and rivers, fished in tributaries, bathed and washed clothes in streams. What salacious beast prowled my subconscious, warning me to be cautious?

Countless galaxies illumined the night when I climbed out of my jeep to open the ranch gate. I searched the sky for some foreshadowing of what was to come, but there was only darkness, flickering pinpricks of light, and the cosmos's untold secrets.

Snuggled in bed, my chilled rump tucked into John's groin, we whispered to each other as an owl called from the spruce tree by the back door and a coyote replied from the river willows.

Interlocking Limbs

Intricate as a Chinese puzzle
our arms and legs cross, linking
in impossibly perfect patterns
throughout the too short night.

How in heaven's name do we fit together?
Your legs long and thin, mine short and heavy,
your arms thick with muscle, mine white and ropy,
your broad back and narrow hips, mine just the
  opposite,
your knobby knees and slender feet, mine fleshy
  round and extra wide.

We twist and turn, still trying to learn
which way's right or what way's wrong,
believing that somehow we'll work it out.
Love me through the conundrums.
Urge me into the delicious point of knowing
for certain that nothing will pull us apart.

From the Ranch to Denver

Before dawn, in the overcast cold, Blue and I hiked up my beloved ridge to offer prayers for safe passage. How I prayed varied each day depending on my mood. At times I prayed to the wind and the stars, or to the coyotes and elk. At times I prayed to the voice within, the eternal guidance system. Most often, addressing prayers to Spirit, my concept of the divine delved into an odd mix of Native American spirituality and New Age universal connection. I still prayed to the Christian trinity of my youth, but only when I attended the Lutheran church with my mother. I believed in anyone or anything that might help me figure out the Gordian knot of life.

"What about you?" I asked Blue as he nudged my knee when I paused on the steep slope. "What do you believe?"

Cocking his ears, he listened, searched my face for the reason why we'd stopped.

"Go on," I said. "It's okay."

He sprang away, running from sagebrush to rabbit brush, sniffing out smells, marking his territory, investigating the world with devoted attention, trying to find out who had passed before him. I admired his ability to be so alive in the moment, without worry, without cares. His thoughts never went beyond bowls of food and water, chasing rabbits, a nap in the sun. His only longings, perhaps, were for an affectionate pat, a belly scratch, kind words, and the honor of following John or me around the ranch.

The Old Ridge Waits

The old ridge waits, a lover in the gloaming dark,
with timbered arms rough, graying, cold, and stark
reached wide and open for my clumsy warm embrace,
my rushed and hurried coming while the day's soft
  face
still slept. I skirt the sage that slows my hastened step
and gallop down a gully where a rabbit leapt
the steep, snowed side to reach the wind-freed
  tangled roots
of trees, and hide there from my heavy, well-worn boots
which run the firm dry dirt that leaves no track or trace
of my sweaty, hot, adolescent, breathless race.

I climb the whiskered scrub-brush of this solemn
  place,
my feet and fingers grabbing kisses without grace,
yet like an aging man who likes a young girl's touch,
the old ridge does not grumble or complain too much.

The day cleared, giving itself over to sun and wind. I finished the housework, made phone calls, and fixed John's favorite hamburgers and fries for lunch to celebrate our last chance to be together.

Seeing my duffle bag and backpack, Blue pouted and refused to look at me. Silent, unsmiling, John didn't make leaving easy, but when I hugged him good-bye, I had a hard time letting go. I felt like a Velcro strip being ripped apart when he pulled away. "Good luck," he said, tucking a brand-new shiny penny into my hand, "and be careful."

I drove out of the ranch, watching the house and barn recede in the rearview mirror, the early afternoon light coloring everything gold. I made one fast stop in town to say good-bye to a friend, giving her a pound of whole-wheat flour I had ground. Feeling my damp palms, noticing my nervousness, she hugged me and said with a big smile, "Laurie, you'll be fine. It's only water."

Clouds drifting up the valley turned fog to drizzle as I headed into Denver. Visibility nonexistent, I coached myself to hold the steering wheel light. Practicing deep breathing, I maneuvered my way through traffic tangles with unskilled luck and arrived at Lana's in time to watch her say good-bye to her college-age son and daughter. She handed them a list of instructions for taking care of the house, then shooed them out the door to go visit their father.

"Hi," she said, "come in."

We walked into the chaos of her trying to clean, do laundry, and pack all at once. "Sorry for the frenzy. It's my life these days," she said, ushering me into a small office. "Sit, relax, we'll talk later, okay?"

I studied the bookshelves and picked up Sor Juana's *Woman of Genius* to read in an attempt to keep my mind off the river. Lana poked her head in the door, "How many pairs of pants are you taking?"

"The brochure said two would be enough," I answered.

She shrugged her shoulders. "Guess I should have read those. No time. Keeping the kids lined out. Work. Trying to find an hour here or there so I can paint. Well, you know how it is? You're an artist, aren't you?"

"Writer," I said. "A poet," I added, hoping that might clarify who I was.

"Should have guessed," she said, smiling. "Listen, I have to go to the store and see some friends. You'll be okay here?"

"Sure. It feels like heaven just to sit here and do nothing."

"Okay then. Back soon."

When the door slammed behind her, the house turned pin-drop quiet. I sat cross-legged on the couch and wrote in my journal: "The river, a different environment, a strange landscape, people I don't know. How will I capture it? I want to write about this, need to take something home to share with everyone who helped me make this journey. Where would I be without them? Where will I find the right words to tell them what happens to me?"

Stopping to think, I fingered the soft edge of the navy blue vest I wore. My father's. Gone almost three years, and still the ache pressed against my chest. If he were here, maybe he could help me figure out what was going on in my life.

My Father's Shirts

I wear my father's shirts and vests
as if the cloth, his second skin,
could shield me from the startled loss
of his fine flesh, his handsome face,
his aged and softened hands.

Amazed that he, so large and big
all the years when I was small,
could nearly be my very size except
for sleeves whose crisp clean cuffs
brush my shaking fingertips.

I wear my father's shirts and vests
as if the warmth of woven wool
could give me back his shoulders strong,
his ready laugh, his loud fast talk,
his boyish quick and caustic wit.

I wear my father's shirts and vests
knowing no one will ever fill
his worn and empty boots.

Rustling in the kitchen cued me that Lana had returned. She appeared, holding a steaming mug.

"Tea?" she asked.

"No, thanks," I said, "I'm fine."

"Did you read any of those books on the Anasazi Expeditions' list of things to read to prepare for the trip?" she asked.

"No," I said, "never did. Never even looked at one. Think I should have?"

"I don't know. Maybe. I intended to. Just never found time."

"Lana, maybe this is foolish, but I wanted to approach this adventure as a novice, as someone unprepared for what might happen. I didn't want the experiences of other people to color the way I might think or feel about the Canyon."

"Interesting premise," she said.

"Here," she added, handing me a coffee table book of Canyon paintings by famous artists, "maybe this will serve as inspiration."

She huffed out a tired sigh and said, "I've got to go finish packing. Are you taking a camera?"

"Yes, a small pocket-size 35mm."

"Crazy, but I'm going to haul my Nikon and all the lenses. I want good photos to paint from."

I set the book back on the bookshelf, stared at the front cover, but did not browse the pages. Could I keep from seeing someone else's vision? Could I begin this journey with my own palette of colors and a clean canvas untouched by anyone else's brush strokes? I picked up my journal and wrote: "Georgia O'Keeffe painted late morning's face with clouds, gunmetal gray over layers of baby blue and virgin white, a violent softness in the sky that highlighted the bones beneath the dark eyebrow of the ridge, an aquiline nose of trees, curved ear of the river, broad grassy cheeks, sharp jawline of lichened rock, the open mouth of my adoration."

"What are you doing," Lana asked, standing in the doorway holding a camera bag.

"Just scribbling."

"Can I see?" she asked.

"Well, no," I said, not wanting to invite any comment, "not right now. It isn't finished."

"I understand," she said. "Sure you'll be comfortable here? Have enough covers?"

"I'm fine," I said, not willing to admit that a knife-sharp fear was stuck in my gut.

"Bathroom's across the hall. See you in the morning. We can talk then?"

"Sounds fine," I said. "Lana, thank you for having me here."

"Hey, no problem. Sleep well."

From Denver to the South Rim of the Grand Canyon

I snuggled into the couch bed surrounded by a halo of light beaming through the small paned windows from the house next door. Comfortable, warm enough in an oversized T-shirt, and covered by a beige duvet, I slept on and off, waking to wander into the bathroom, or tiptoe around Lana's living room to study her paintings barely visible in the bluish glow of streetlights. Her work reflected her scattered high-energy intensity and attention to minute details.

Wide-awake, I squirmed around in my self-made nest and tried to calm the edgy uneasiness that kept me from resting. An insistent clock ticked its torture until I called upstairs to Lana, heard her stirring, turning on the shower. After dressing in river pants, hiking boots, a quick-drying shirt, and a nylon windbreaker, I concocted a breakfast of bananas, granola, nuts, and raisins left out on the kitchen counter. Lana rushed past, putting on the kettle, doing laundry, setting out the garbage, taking care of the cat, using the phone, making more lists. Breathless in the cold predawn air, she piled our gear in her SUV.

The interstate, brilliant wet with black glare from rain in the night, sported traffic zinging along bumper to bumper. Lana's speed, coupled with red taillights, white headlights, onrushing lights, lights, and more lights moving like cascading water, unnerved my pretense of tranquility. Long ensconced on the ranch, not prepared for the city's confusion, I clenched my jaws to keep from screaming.

An hour later, Lana pulled into the airport. In that short amount of time I knew I had shed a decaying layer of skin. The restless ranch wife was gone. In her place stood a woman, tiptoe on a ledge, arms outstretched, face lifted to the sky.

Change of Heart

She spits the tit from her sucking mouth,
turns her face away from spoon-fed pabulum,
the cooing words she once worshipped,
and nods acquiescence to the next woman
who will redden her knees kneeling,
fingering the tongue of a zipper like a rosary,
waiting for an answer to a prayer that is not there.

What happens when a woman finally grows up,
quits playing the dutiful daughter or the happy
    housewife?
She stretches her legs in the sun and eats avocados.
She grows lilies and lilacs and learns to speak Spanish.
She listens to a heart that's exercising and losing weight.
She loves every mangy cat that happens to come along
and winks at herself each morning in the bathroom
    mirror.

Checking in at the ticket counter, the agent eyed our bags and said, "You can only take one bag each on board. One that fits under the seat or in the overhead compartment."

"We're headed for a river trip and need this gear with us," Lana explained.

"No way, ladies. It's a rule," he said.

"No way, sir. We take our stuff with us or find another airline that will accommodate us," Lana said.

"Fine. Fine," he responded to her tone of voice and flung up his hands. "Go talk to the gate agent."

We humped our heavy bags down the corridor. "That took guts," I said.

"Geez," Lana wheezed as we sweated our way to the gate. "It's a pain to have to get pushy."

"Hey, there," she said to the woman behind the counter, "we need our bags with us."

"So I heard," the agent said, tagging our bags for immediate pickup at our arrival gate in Las Vegas.

Boarding the flight, two attendants debated the legality of having our bags on board. The duffles and backpacks disappeared from the end of the jet way.

"Oops," I said, "I bet that's the last we see of them."

"Damn regulations," Laura said. "Oh, come on, let's not worry about it."

Crowded, the plane hummed with the noise of other voices, but Lana and I talked, half-shouting to be heard.

"I wasn't sure how I felt about traveling with a woman I didn't know," I volunteered.

"I know," she laughed, her frank blue eyes widening along with her smile. "It's tricky. What if we hated each other from the start?"

"Thank goodness that's not the case. I can tell you right

now I like your openness, your tough-girl way of dealing with things, and your paintings," I said.

"That's a relief," she said. "There's nothing worse than being disliked or criticized. So, tell me about you, the ranch, your husband. John, right? What's he like? Mine was a real strange study."

"John's, well, John is John. There's no one else like him in the world. He's like a throwback to another era and maybe God broke the mold when he made him. He's honest and hard-working, has old-fashioned values, is a good neighbor, generous with his kids, kind with the animals," I said.

"You make him sound like the hero in a bad Western," Lana said. "That's the sugarcoating. What's he really like?"

"Okay," I said. "Let's see if I can paint a more complete picture. He's quiet, a loner, impossibly stubborn, set in his ways, hates the modern world, says people are no damn good, holds a grudge forever, doesn't know how forgiveness works, loves me but isn't very good at showing it, and right now is probably nursing the hurt of me leaving by working himself into the ground," I said.

"He sounds wonderful to me," she said. "Is he handsome?"

"Yes," I said, wanting to tease her along, "a dreamboat."

Lana laughed, the intense, unsmiling, preoccupied woman of the night before dissolving before my eyes.

"What's he look like?" she asked.

"John's tall, over six foot, lean and wiry from working so much, never wears anything but Levi's and boots, has big blue eyes, a drooping silver mustache, and beautiful hands," I said.

"Geez," she said. "Is there anything wrong with this man?"

"Well, he never goes anywhere without his hat, he cusses a lot, he's obsessed with the Weather Channel, intimacy eludes him, and he hates poetry," I said.

"Uh-oh," Lana said.

"Anything else?" she asked.

"He's going bald," I offered.

We laughed together. "Tell me about your husband," I said.

"Ex-husband," Lana said. "He drank. He drinks. I mean he has a problem with, oh never mind. Let's not talk about husbands anymore."

Flight Delayed

Her wrinkled winnie-pooh pillow breaks over
the hard arm of the airport's crummy metal chair
and touches the gray pebbled carpet of the floor,
her face half hidden by a chin length bob of hair.

She sleeps, a mystery of soft-shut childish eyes,
with thin shaped brows and tiny nose above arched
    lip,
a trio of gold rings weave through her seashell ear,
a tiny mole marks her rounded exposed hip.

Beltless too-big jeans encase coltish legs that cross
at sockless bony ankles strapped inside worn shoes,
her Christmas colored sweater rises high in back
revealing skin and a surprising glimpse of clues:

A boy's broad band of underwear, black signed on
    white,
"Tommy" printed boldly upon elastic line,
and clutched in hand upon her small flat lap, a wad
of yellow roses fading fast from bright and fine.

Tied up with silver ribbon dying blooms dismiss
my first interpretation of her gilded youth,
wild girl gone over to the world of womanhood
without license purchased to turn her from her
    truth.

She wakes from rest as startled as a cross fox kit
caught in the secret headlights of a midnight trip,
yet stretching hard she yawns and arches satisfied
and licks away the dream left hanging on her lip.

As I watched the young woman across the aisle in the Las Vegas terminal, Lana sat on the floor going through her gear.

"Hi, guys," we heard and turned to see Angie walking up with two other women.

"Angie," I shouted and jumped up to hug her.

Her lithe body rigid, her smile distant, she asked, "How are you?"

"Fine," I lied, and backed away as everyone else hugged, exchanging greetings, their intercourse transforming me into an outsider because the other women all knew each other.

"Is everyone else feeling as off center and out of balance as I am?" Angie asked.

"Yes," I said. "Would someone please tell me why all of you packed light and sensible, while my big duffle feels like a Mack truck?"

Lana picked up her camera case. One of the zoom lenses fell and cracked on the uncarpeted floor.

"Shit," she said, her expression revealing frustration. "There goes my next paycheck."

"Oh, let's get a grip," Helen said. "If you're all struggling like I am, then we're all in this together. We might as well make it fun."

She raised her sunglasses in a mock salute and added, "Here's to the unknown."

At the Scenic Air counter, the agent cracked jokes. "I rafted the river two weeks ago," he said, laughing. "Let me tell you about Lava Falls and my middle-of-the-night encounter with a scorpion."

"Is that supposed to give us courage?" Lana asked.

"Oh, you don't need courage," he said. "Only fools and visionaries return unscathed."

He held out his hand for Lana's camera and took our photo: five women, five backpacks, five duffles, five trying-to-be-brave smiles.

A minibus shuttled us from the main airport to the Scenic Air terminal. The downtown strip assaulted me: snarled ropes of slow traffic, gawking tourists, enough glitz to glaze over eyes in seconds.

"How's John doing?" Angie asked.

"Fine, like always," I snapped.

Then, needing to apologize, I added, "Sorry, Angie. I'm operating on overload. I just want to be back on the ranch hiking with Blue. And I'm nervous about making the duffle drop-off time. Do you have the number to call ahead and alert Bright Angel Lodge that we're behind schedule but on our way?"

In-flight headphones provided both Japanese and English guided tours as we soared to the South Rim, but listening bored me, and the plane's tiny porthole windows allowed only a token glimpse of the landscape. I shucked my hiking boots and wandered barefoot from row to row trying to take in the entire visual feast. Smashing my big toe into a steel seat leg, I plopped back down to watch it swell into a purple-black egg.

"Well, this is an inauspicious start," I complained to Gina across the aisle.

When she didn't reply, I looked up to see her bent over, her face pale.

"Are you all right?" I asked.

"I've never been airsick before," she said.

I shimmied over and rubbed her back. "Just breathe," I said. "Take deep breaths."

First off the plane, Angie arranged our cab ride to the South Rim. Cluttered with tourist stuff, the area advertised the fact that 22,000 people a year go down the river and thousands more visit the Canyon for sightseeing and hiking.

"Why," I moaned to Angie, "did I think it would be rustic and unspoiled?"

Stuck in the back of a shuttle van listening to a too-loud radio and six voices talking at once, I longed for an hour alone up on my ridge. Most misery loved company, but this misery wanted solitude, wanted out of the van, out of Arizona, and out of this insane trip. I pressed my lips together to keep from saying so.

Jammed shoulder to shoulder at the Bright Angel Lodge, we stood in line with our gear for a late check-in.

I groaned when the woman behind the counter reported, "Your duffle is eighteen pounds; day pack thirteen."

Lana laughed, "It could be worse. At least a mule is going to pack your duffle down."

Helen panicked when she couldn't find the rolls of film she had bought. Spreading her stuff out on the lobby floor, she searched without success through every pocket and cubbyhole. Sensing her disquiet, unable to breathe in the crowded room, I pushed my way outside to perch on the low, rock wall overlooking the Canyon. People pushed past, loud voices echoed everywhere. Gina walked up and put her hand on my shoulder.

"Okay?" she asked.

"Not really," I said, presenting a small smile. "I feel like I'm being pulled in twenty ways at once, but I'll survive. Look at the buttes and mesas, the variegated colors, the resplendent horizon."

Gina looked a long time, then said, "Angie told me you were a poet."

I laughed. "That was more cliché than poetry, but now I have an inkling of why I had to come on this trip."

"I know," she said, the brisk breeze bringing some color back into her face. "And, Laurie, just think, we haven't even started yet."

Helen and Angie agreed to room together. That left me to share with Lana and Gina. We clustered in the doorway to survey the large room with a double bed, a single bed, and an old-fashioned bathroom with a seductive claw-foot tub.

Watching Angie walk away with Helen sent the hot scrape of being deserted prickling across my shoulders. I shrugged it off. I'd been wrong to assume Angie and I would bunk with one another. She was friends with all of us. It was okay.

The envy returned, settling with sharp claws. No, it wasn't okay. I needed her. Besides, I'd known her longer than the others.

Ravenous irritation dug in.

"Oh, go away," I said, shrugging harder.

"What did you say, Laurie?" Gina asked.

"Nothing. Just that it's been a long day."

We hiked up the path along the South Rim to El Tovar, arriving only ten minutes late for our dinner reservation.

"Elegant," I said to Lana. "I feel really out of place in these baggy pants, wrinkled shirt, and ball cap."

"Handsome, huh?" Lana whispered when our waiter appeared.

"What will it be, ladies?" he asked, presenting a royal bow.

"We need calories," Angie stated.

"Going down the trail?" he asked.

"Yes," we answered in unison and rattled off salmon, swordfish, salad, corn chowder, bruschetta.

While waiting for entrees, we ate buttered rolls and

drank endless glasses of water as Angie coached us, "Hydrate, girls, hydrate. It's going to be a long hike."

When the busboy cleared our plates, the waiter appeared with a crème brûlée and five dessertspoons.

"On the house," he said, "and good luck."

Passing the plate around the table, we each took bites. Helen said, "cool," Angie offered "sweet," Gina said "smooth," Lana presented "like silk," and I added, "yes, like silk sheets on a hot summer night."

"That figures," she laughed, "the poet upstages the painter."

Thanking us for joining her on the journey, Angie picked up the tab. We strolled into the I-wish-I-had-a-jacket-on night air to find the Bright Angel trailhead. Fatigue and stress acted like too much tequila in our systems. Giddy, stumbling in the darkness, we all talked at once.

A small store, still open near the lodge, provided oranges and bananas for our breakfasts. As we dragged back to our rooms, I begged Lana and Gina, "Please let me have the single bed. If I don't sleep, I won't make the hike down."

"Grovel," Lana teased.

"Okay," I said, "I promise you both a foot rub if you acquiesce."

"Done deal," Lana said as Gina grinned approval.

Taking my turn in the claw-foot tub, I scalded my sore foot by turning on the hot water faucet with my toes. "I'm such a fool," I muttered, "I should be going through this unscathed."

Portrait of a Woman in Her Bath

Blood-tinged discharge seeps from her,
surrounds her fine dun hair which floats
like seaweed in the shallows of a night too long.

Maroon thins ethereally to pink in the warm wash
of water that faucet-spills over her large feet,
splashing the pale islands of bent knees and breasts.

Her eyes close. Buoyant, freed, her arms lift away
from her heavy thighs, embrace the ancient
solace of emptiness, the constellation of silence.

Her pulse softens and slows, stutters once, starts,
then stops. Ichor runs in her veins for one still
moment until she remembers, suddenly, to breathe.

Below Hermit Rapids on the Colorado River

Cuddling a strange pillow, I slept with earplugs to block out background noise.

Way before first light, I dressed, then stretched to prepare for the hike, ate two oranges and tanked up on water. When Gina stirred, I said, "You were up and down quite a few times."

"I don't feel very well," she said.

"Do you live at sea level?" I asked.

"Yes, not far from the coast."

"Then you might have altitude sickness. I think Angie said it was over seven thousand feet here," I said.

"Well, Miss Restless and Ready to Go," Lana said on her way to the bathroom, "what time is it anyway?"

"Four-fifteen," I said, "I thought we better get an early start."

She yawned. "It's only nine and a half miles. We'll be fine."

"I hope so," I said, "Fatigue is already sucking at my ability to go that far."

"Call up willpower," she said. "You don't have a choice now."

Looking at my watch for the last time, I wrapped it with my airline tickets and wallet in a plastic bag and tucked them into my fanny pack.

Helen and Angie joined us. They looked cute in their caps and packs with water bottles hanging off their belts.

As we gathered up our gear, Lana asked, "How old is everyone?"

"Forty-four," Angie said.

"Forty-nine," Gina answered.

"Fifty-six," Helen said, and we all cheered.

"Laurie?" Lana asked.

"Forty-six," I replied.

"Well, that makes us almost sisters. I'm forty-seven."

Before a hint of dawn colored the sky, we headed toward the trailhead, a gaggle of girls preening new feathers, laughing and talking.

Portrait of a Woman at a Window

From where she watches, patient dawn braids
a salmon ribbon in the horizon's fair hair and the
    pines
are black lace stretched over the white skin of the sky.

She wears only a long T-shirt that reaches to her knees
and her limbs, bare and cold, curl toward her heart's
    heat,
curl her into silence, her emptiness that is full of peace.

Her eyes, still heavy with sleep, close, and she cradles
her small breasts, breathes evenly so her child-like
    breath
creates milk-white whorls on the cool, paned glass.

This is the sole moment when she is most herself,
content to watch the day create itself, surprised to
    find
when she opens her eyes, a world of light and
    possibility.

The voice of the Canyon rose out of the surrounding rock and I longed for quiet to hear what she had to say. The sky wasn't pitch black, but it was difficult to see. Helen and Gina used flashlights to find their footing, but the bright beams felt disruptive and out of place. I stayed at the back of our pack, searching for signs of the ancient ones who had guarded the Canyon for so long.

I prayed, "Spirit, give me strength. Grant me peace of mind. Help me keep my emotions stable. I don't think I can do this alone. Help me find my way."

I placed one foot with care in front of the other, feeling my way because I could not see, trusting my ears and nose to guide me. The pungent odor of equine urine rose from puddles left when the mules had gone down the trail with our duffles in the middle of the night. At each switchback, I offered up the short prayer, "Let me honor the sacredness of this place and time."

Hiking down the Bright Angel Trail, a friend had told me, was like going back into the womb of the earth. She was right. Going down into the darkness moved me as I trusted invisible guides swishing past me in the thin air. Above tower-like cliffs, the sky stretched gray-black, the stars scintillant. I stared at the spot where we started just minutes before. A gradual, tarnished silver glow turned the canyon walls nearly white with a slow brightening, an exquisite quickening.

The poetry of the place embraced me, but, as I'd heard many say, it was a struggle to find the right words to describe it. After many inadequate attempts, I conjured thoughts of every imaginary lover I'd ever had and believed I could come close to describing the incredible sensation if I combined the passion of them all.

A too-many-people-and-too-many-voices confusion tipped

my balance, making me crave an impossible aloneness.

Down, down, down. Step by step. Steep, unscalable walls on one side, sheer drop-offs on the other. Mule droppings marked the trail, and the rubber-shod tracks holding glimmers of urine showed the way. Fussy as a penned mule, I wished I'd gone down the trail with them instead of with the girls.

First Sight

In the quick minutes just before dawn
the first strong brush strokes of sun
paint the white face of Coconino sandstone.

Like a school of pilot fish in a cobalt sea,
minute pink clouds swim across the sky,

Brush and rocks and trees materialize
out of darkness into the light of day.

The miracle triggers a rush of sweet love.
Quick and sudden, I fall, weak in the knees.

Time snaked by as the first mile and a half of the trail disappeared behind us. Gina, pale again, sighed that she was dizzy. I offered my bottled electrolytes and Angie stayed with her to maintain a slow, but steady pace. Concerned that we might miss the boats, I pushed into the lead and hustled, Lana and Helen right behind me. Reaching the three-mile rest stop, I pulled off the trail to see the far view and left a hasty prayer floating into the upper branches of a giant gnarled tree. Then, dogtrotting, I caught up with Helen and Lana.

Others joined us on the trail. Those going down at a fast pace passed us and those coming up looked weary and unhappy, their faces serious from the strenuous climb. A third of the way down the trail, bunched tightness tore at my calves and my sore foot throbbed.

Angie and Gina caught up at the oasis of Indian Gardens where a stream, shouldered with shadows, spilled through uneven rocks.

"Your eyes look brighter," I said to Gina. "Feeling better?"

"Yes, and I'll feel even better when I use this bathroom."

Waiting for my turn, I changed into dry socks and put moleskin on toe and heel hot spots.

"We better hurry," I said as Helen, Gina, and Lana snapped group photos.

The Canyon widened with changing views that presented an endless array of colors and textures, an infinite sky, the remote horizon, the cliffs so high I stretched my neck backwards like a ballerina to see the heights. Two mule deer browsed brush on the edge of the trail, one a fawn, the other a doe with her ribs showing. Unperturbed, ears flapping back and forth, black tails swishing, they nibbled, then chewed, jaws grinding as they stopped to gaze at us.

Down I hiked, toes and hips hurting. The shade of Canyon walls provided relief from the sapping heat. Bathed in sweat, my body said drink often, my mind said save your water. Snapping my ball cap onto my belt, I used a cooler bandanna for a headband. Helen stopped with me in the middle of a soothing creek crossing.

"What would we do if it was the middle of summer?" she asked.

The Earth Is Honest

The earth is honest in her undertakings.
whoever she is in the moment,
whatever she does,
she never lies.

She is certain of her business
and of her significant place
in the center of all things.

This is her truth:
the sharp slap of wind,
a single shaft of sun
shot through a hole in storm clouds,
the arrow of her power
piercing my heart.

I never thought to keep count of other hikers on the trail. Perhaps we passed fifty or more. Some, young and athletic, danced down the trail like mountain goats. Some, older, but still agile and spry, walked with stalwart purpose. A few, overweight and huffing, carried strain in their heavy eyes and tight lips. While some walked freehanded, many others used spiked walking sticks. Some sported only a knapsack and water bottle, and some labored under full packs. Most were hiking from the North Rim to the South Rim. "Good mornings" were exchanged, but intent on their own journeys, no one stopped to talk.

A teenage couple that had flown down the trail hours earlier, now climbed their way back. The boy recognized us and said, "Ten more minutes and you'll see the river!"

Reaching Pipe Creek Beach, where the light-green Colorado ran smooth and easy in a great glistening expanse of water, we whooped in a circle, hugging each other.

We hiked around the corner, cliff walls on one side, and the incomparable river on the other. On mostly level ground, the trail quartered up the Canyon to a gigantic silver bridge that carried foot traffic across the river and supported the main water line to the South Rim. Close now, anticipating the end of our hike, we passed stone barns and mule corrals and spotted two guys pushing and pulling a child-size Anasazi Expeditions wagon loaded with water cans.

"We picked up your duffles at the hitching post," one shouted. "They're at the beach."

Hot in the sun, we trudged after them through sand surrounded by feathery-leafed tamarisk trees. Seeing the sign for Phantom Ranch, I longed to explore, but there was no time and, besides, I was fading and desperate for a nap.

Catnap

Outside, sitting in the sun on a windowsill,
the cat cleans her paws, stretching out her claws
to lick the little folds of skin that connect
the gray, grainy pads of her feet
before she curls into an "O" and sleeps.

Inside, resting in a rectangle of window-filtered light,
I clip my nails to nubs then rub coconut cream
between and over each cracked finger
before I stretch out into an "X"
and close my eyes to sleep.

Twenty-eight people jostled for space on a slice of beach where six moored, light-blue boats bobbed. I swallowed, my heart skipping one long beat. There were way too many people going on the river. Our trip leader, Robb, introduced himself and asked our names. Then, he repeated them back, pointing to each of us in turn.

"Impressive," I said to Lana.

"I know," she said, "and he didn't even mix us up when we're both blonde and our names are similar."

"Okay," Robb said. "We dropped off eight women who hiked out via Bright Angel. You probably passed them on the way down. We've got nine new members. That means less space and that you guys brought too much stuff."

Lana nudged me and I blushed.

Instructing us to repack our duffle gear, Robb gave each of us a black rubber sack and a smaller blue bag for the things we would need during the day on the boats.

"These will keep your gear dry if you pack them right. We'll hand out your sleep kits and tents when we stop for the night," he said.

Tired and disgruntled, I labored to organize my stuff and jam everything into two bags. One of the boatmen heard me grumbling and strolled over.

"Here," he said, "push the air out like this, roll the top, then strap it down to keep everything waterproof."

"Thanks," I said, offering him my hand. "You are?"

"Shane," he said.

"Thanks again, Shane."

"Hey, no problem, that's what we're here for.

"Go ahead and keep your backpack with you," he added. "You can use it to store your hiking boots. Make sure you put them in a plastic bag, though."

Zipping off my pants legs to make shorts, I sat in the

sand, tried to catch my breath and calm down.

"Okey-dokey," Robb called. "Listen up. Lesson on hygiene. Pee in the river, not on the ground. The river can handle the influx of urine better than the fragile environment of the beaches. Don't poop in the river or on the ground. Use the groovers. They will be set up every evening on each end of camp with a signal cushion on the path. If the cushion's gone, groover's occupied. If it's there, the place is all yours. If you have any questions about any of this, come and see me."

A friend had told me: Leave your underwear at home. It's easier and faster to pee if you don't have to deal with an extra layer of clothing. Searching, I found a scant patch of pale-colored brush, struggled out of my shorts, took off my beige lace-edged panties, and stuffed them into a pocket, slipped my shorts back on and sat in the sand once more to strap on my Tevas for the first time.

Waving Gina and Helen over, we made our way upriver around a bunch of boulders to wade out where it was more private. Helen giggled like a grade school girl.

"Remember how your mother always said, 'Don't pee in the swimming pool.' I feel like I'm breaking a rule," she said.

"New rules," I said, feeling my warm, sharp-smelling urine trickle into the cool water. The two mixed, swirling around my legs as I swiveled my hips to rinse. My wet nylon shorts clung to my thighs as I stepped from the river onto rounded rocks.

"I don't know about you," I added, stepping with care from boulder to boulder, "but I feel unencumbered. Light, airy. At ease."

Day of the Week

Remember day of the week panties
a different color for every day
pink for Monday, blue for Tuesday,
green Wednesday, yellow Thursday,
purple Friday, red Saturday,
white Sunday.

The names of the days
spelled out in script
just above the right thigh
as if you could just lift your skirt
and said "yes, it's Monday . . .
that means math and biology"
or "it's Sunday, sorry no sex."

Opening an underwear drawer
in a hurry, searching through
all those days and colors
looking for answers
and finally you just grabbed any pair
and put them on.

What a silly ploy to keep girls organized.
It calls for a subversive act:
we won't wear panties at all.

The Anasazi Expeditions crew set up a table in the shade and laid out lunch. Standing in line, I tried to identify each member: Robb, Hank, Stefan, Shane, Meg. I couldn't recall the names of the couple running one of the baggage boats. Making a sandwich with whole wheat bread, lettuce and tomatoes, mayonnaise, I added chips and a couple of cookies to round out my meal. Meg handed out gray plastic mugs to be used every day for coffee, lemonade, soup, and water. When Lana used a black marker to draw a Canyon scene on her cup, I begged her to decorate mine too.

"What do you want?" she asked.

"Something peaceful."

"You got it," she said, and sketched in a stretch of calm water and the edge of a cliff.

Fast-paced and confusing, minutes zipped past as the crew repacked the boats. Kindergartner shy, I waited by my gear. Shane came over, tightened a last stubborn strap, and handed me a marker.

"Write your name on those pieces of duct tape on front of the bags," he said. "Then, pass it on."

Robb waved the newcomers into a group by a pile of faded orange life jackets.

"All right," he said, "these are your new best friends. Everybody pick one. Don't go anywhere without it. When you're on the boat, it's on you. When you're off the boat, clip it to a strap to keep the wind from stealing it. When you get off the boat at night take it to bed with you. Buddy up because it will be the only thing to save your life. We'll put your name or number on the back. Remember which one is yours and keep it close."

Pulling a life jacket from the stack, I caught a glimpse of two sevens barely visible on the back. I smiled at my lucky roll of the dice. Sevens could only mean good fortune and a safe journey. Robb used his black marker to write people's names on the backs of their jackets, but I turned away. I didn't want my name on the personal floatation device. The double seven would keep me from harm. Shane stepped up to snug my straps. I raised my arms skyward as I'd seen Lana do, and he tugged the six black bands tight.

"I can't breathe," I said.

"It needs to be tight so it won't slip off in a rapid," he explained, but he loosened each by a hair's breadth.

Feeling like a bulky corset was hugging me, I welcomed the jacket's embrace.

"Instructions on river protocol," Robb said. "Number one: Introduce yourselves."

We all laughed, said our names, shook hands, asked, "Where are you from?" I did my mental exercises, but after Nick and Suzanne from Massachusetts, who had hiked down the Kaibab Trail with all their gear on their backs, and Daniel, a teacher from Illinois, I lost the rest of the names. We stood looking awkward in our shorts, river sandals, and life vests with the sun beating down on us.

"Number two: Always wear shoes."

I grinned. He stood there barefoot in the sand with red ants crawling all over his feet and up his legs.

He laughed.

"Do as I say and not as I do. The ants bite if they are trapped between your foot and sandal, but otherwise they are harmless. They come out during the day, but go in at night. During the day, watch for red racers and rattlesnakes. At night the scorpions skulk about."

He paused, looking around, then shouted, "Hey, Caleb, Scorp King, come here. Tell the folks what happened to you the other night."

Looking like he loved being center stage, Caleb jogged

over and said, "I gathered up my gear one rainy night to go sleep in the shelter of a rock cave and put my hand down on a scorpion in the dark."

We gathered close to stare at the still-swollen palm of his hand.

"Did it hurt?" Lana asked.

"Not much," he answered. "The sting made me feel a bit wired and out of sorts for a couple of days, but no long-term aftereffects."

"There's nothing deadly poisonous in the Canyon," Robb said. "Please, if you see a snake or a scorpion, don't smash it and mash it on the rocks. Come get one of us and we'll remove it to a safe place. They live here. We are just guests.

"Next lesson," Robb said as he waved us over to one of the boats and demonstrated the proper way to ride.

"Plant your butt on the rounded side of the boat and sit deep, grab the handhold strap. Set your feet firm and flat on the bottom of the boat to ride out the rapids. If the boat dumps, let go. Close your mouth. If you go under, re-member to close your mouth so you don't take in any water and swim toward the light. Boats rarely dump, but if one does, your life jacket will keep you afloat until another boat comes to pull you back in."

Robb shifted his weight and shook the ants from his feet. He lifted his white straw cowboy hat, scooped back his black hair then settled his hat again.

"Any questions?" he asked. We shook our heads no.

Squinting into the sun, he said, "Okey-dokey, let's go."

Red Ants

They swirl out of the sand
confronting the boatman's bare feet
each tanned toe a mountain to ascend
the round boulder of ankle
the curved cliffs of his calves
the knobby outcropping of his knees.

They begin their studious ascent
by following each other over
the slick slide rock of nails,
the crevices between toes.

The boatman shifts his weight
and lightly shakes his leg.
The ants fall gentle to the sand,
reconnoiter, and begin to climb again.

Waiting at the boat with Robb's name on front, I hung back watching as Angie and Gina crawled over gear to the stern, and Lana and Helen took the two seats in front. Last in the bow, I looked around for something to hold on to.

"Here, Laurie," Helen said, pointing to a black webbed strap secured to the boat by a metal ring, "hold on to this."

I laughed and said, "I'd rather hold on to Robb."

With a tight throat and clammy hands, foreboding shadowed me like a thundercloud. Robb pulled a steel stake out of the sand and coiled the bowline, knotted the loops loosely, then tossed the rope into a five-gallon bucket near my feet. He shoved off and leapt onto the boat.

For a second his hand settled on my shoulder, calming me. Steering the boat into the main current, he manipulated the long oars with casual ease and we were swept into a large rapid. The first wave reared over my head and crashed down. Not having enough sense to turn my face away or close my gaping mouth, I spat water and screamed.

Holding my black strap like a bareback rider, taking a deep seat, I went for the eight-second whistle. The boat bucked through waves and rollers, reared high, fishtailed down. Dripping wet, smiling, sheer radiance beamed all around me. Behind us the rapid looked small and unthreatening. I loosened my death grip on the strap, realizing that when the first sparkling wave washed over me, my fear of the river disappeared.

"Eh-haw," Robb said in a long, soft, drawn-out sigh.

We replied with exuberance, "EH-HAW," and our female voices rang from the walls.

Horn Creek Rapid

The approach to the white water is smooth, jade
  green and glassy.
Twin bulges of water rise from the sides of the river's
  forehead.

The boatman eases the blue raft in sideways between
  the bright horns,
then turns bow first into the curling waves of rushing
  spray and foam.

For a moment we are lost in a devilish maw,
churned and chewed, rolled in a roar of angry water

that spits us out on the other side like a piece of
  driftwood.

After that first rapid, Robb said, "Time to learn to bail."

He pointed to buckets clipped with carabiners in the front and back of each boat. Smaller split plastic bottles with handles served as scoops.

"River rule," he said. "The boatman puts the water in and the riders bail the water out."

It was an awkward process. We scooped and threw water with haphazard eagerness, splashing each other, and in the process pouring most of the water back in the boat. Robb laughed at us.

"Helen," I said, pushing her away, "you just dumped part of a bucket right in my lap."

"It takes time, but you'll learn the right routine," Robb said.

Lana and I took turns pressing our feet together to pull all the water into a puddle, then we scooped with syncopated rhythm to fill the big bucket, and Helen dumped it overboard.

"Return to the river what is hers," I said.

"That's nice," Robb said.

"You know what, I like bailing," I said. "It makes me move, and besides, doing this small service makes me feel like I'll earn part of my supper tonight. What I don't like is being bent over with my head between my knees so I can't see a thing but the bottom of the boat. I'm afraid I'll miss something."

"So," Robb said, "what do you all do?"

Lana answered, "I'm an artist." Then, pointing at each of us in turn, she said, "Poet, hospice volunteer, illustrator, writer."

Robb nodded. Then asked, "How'd you all meet?"

"Angie and I lived with the same man," I said.

"At the same time?" he asked, grinning.

"No," I laughed, "four months apart."

"I'm Angie's cousin," Lana said.

"I used to be her next-door neighbor," Helen said.

"Our mothers are best friends," Gina said.

"In other words," I added, "this is all Angie's fault."

Bouncing and bucking through another rapid, we spotted Stefan's boat becalmed in the swirling water of a huge eddy. Robb instructed us, "Here's what we do. Take up the chant 'Stefan's in an eddy.' "

"Stefan's in an eddy," we sang out the childish taunt. "Stefan's in an eddy."

But Stefan, grinning good-naturedly, pulled back on his oars with firm strokes and willed his boat back into the main current.

"That was cruel," Gina said.

"Just camaraderie," Angie said.

"Well," Robb said, "we tease each other all the time. It's a thing between boatmen."

"Like what," Lana asked, "one-upmanship?"

"Maybe it's meant to be supportive and conciliatory in a fun way," I said.

The other boats pulled to the side of the river in slower water, allowing Robb to take the lead. Respect and honor hovered in the air as they waited for us to pass.

"It feels like you're being saluted," I said.

He nodded his head, looked at the sky, then back at the other boats falling into line behind him.

The day turned still and silent except for the sip and swish of oars.

"How long have you been on the river?" I asked Robb.

"Sixteen years," he said.

"How old are you?" I pestered.

"Laurie!" Angie said.

69

Robb hesitated, but replied, "I turned thirty-eight on September twelfth."

"A Virgo," I said," that's why you appear so grounded and calm."

"Really?" he said, tipping his hat back.

"Virgos are clear thinkers. They are practical, courteous, like being of service to others, and practice self-honesty," I said.

"Not me. That sounds like a saint," Robb said. "Anything else?"

"They get cranky when they don't get their own way," I said.

He laughed like he knew what I was talking about.

"How many trips do you do every year?" I asked.

"Between ten and twelve," he said.

Doing easy math, I calculated, then said, "You've encountered the Canyon over a hundred and sixty times."

"Guess so," he said.

"No wonder it seems like you and the river are longtime lovers," I said.

Lana leaned over and whispered to me, "You're quite the tease."

"What do you mean?" I asked.

She didn't answer. She turned around and fished in her dry bag for her camera.

Romancing the River

Until I have felt underfoot her every curve and bend
and heard the sound of her rippled voice
changing from chute to riffle to pool where willows
drape reflections of her thousand faces,
how can I say I know her?

Until I have whispered to her in wonder, stretched
out open on her soft and grassy sides or reached shyly
into the unknown clefts of her undercut banks
and delved the old mysteries of her wild running,
how can I say I want her?

Until I have met and mastered the minds
of other worshippers, occult osprey, reclusive brown,
flash fire of leaping rainbow and hidden heron who
rises from the water phoenix-like, a cloud of mystic
    smoke,
how can I say I accept her?

Until I have walked alongside her in every waking
hour, dawn through dusk, and longer still, night into
    day,
and seen her dark flanks caressed by sun, silvered
    with
starlight and drank mesmerized from her secret
    springs,
how can I say I understand her?

71

Until I have held the haunting silence of her winter
heart in my shaking hands, counted the quick pulsed
flood of spring awakening, yearned for the ripe beauty
of her summer dress and coveted her autumn glory,
how can I say I possess her?

An hour or two is never enough. Even offering
one day diminishes the devotion she so deserves.
Until I plunge into giving everything, vulnerable,
as naked and unashamed as her own soul,
how can I say I love her?

The rapids: Horn, Salt Creek, Granite, Hermit. The wildlife: great blue herons, a bighorn ewe, then later a ram and a ewe browsing together along the cliff edge, pale brown and buff coloring blending into the rock. The scenery kept me searching for words.

After Hermit Rapids we pulled into a sandy beach to camp. The sun disappeared as fast as a secret wink. Robb unloaded first, so I was able to snag my bags and find a secluded spot to camp. I had chosen "The Crystal Palace" out of a stack of canvas tent bags, but didn't set it up. Instead, I laid out my tarp, pad, and sleeping bag.

Our small group went way down the river to wash. I stripped off my sweaty clothes, plunged in and dunked, scrubbed my hair and shaved my legs, then scrambled up onshore to shiver and thaw out before plunging back, dunking again and again to rinse away the biodegradable camp suds. Alarmingly cold, the river's energetic current pulsed around me, her song under the surface of the green water sung by a voice I'd known a long time ago. "He's coming," I heard. "He's coming to you."

Drying off, I asked Angie, "Don't you think the river has her own culture and language?"

"Sure," she said, "a language we need to learn fast in order to stop being such a bunch of greenhorns."

"All right," I said, "correct me if I'm wrong. The members of the crew are boatmen, or as Robb said, 'river scum.' They use oars, not paddles, to maneuver the boats through the water. Each rafting company has different colored boats. Anasazi Expeditions' boats are baby-blue. Each man's boat is his home, therefore inviolate."

"So far so good," Angie laughed. "You sound like you're giving a lecture."

"Where do they keep their gear?" Helen asked. "They

73

don't have dry bags like we do."

"Stored in waterproof ammunition cans strapped to the sides of the well," Gina said.

"What's a well?" I asked.

"Where the boatman sits or stands in the center," she answered. "And, by the way, boatmen row their boats. They do not paddle. Paddling is a term reserved for canoeing and kayaking."

"How do you know all this?" I asked.

"I read the books," she said. "Anyway, each boat contains coolers and boxes that carry the food and supplies needed for the entire trip. The boatmen sleep on their boats, placing pads on the bow cross-board and unrolling their sleeping bags there. If it rains, they throw on a tarp. If it storms, they set up small tents."

"You know what I love," I said. "The river words. Like boils, whirlpools, eddies, rapids. And the rapids have center tongues and laterals, as well as holes, rocks, walls, and white water. I love these words. They feel funny on my tongue. They roll around and around in my mouth until I can taste them."

"No wonder you're a poet," Lana said. "Where did you hear all that?"

"Listening to Caleb talking to the other kayakers," I said.

"Ah, Caleb's cute," she said. "Caleb has possibilities."

Carabiner

It took me forever
to learn how to say it
and I still haven't learned
how to spell it.

Before the river
I didn't even know what it was
they just sent me a list
that said bring one, so I did.

A friend gave me one of his
so mine was second hand
not new and shiny
like some of them.

But I came to care for my carabiner
loving how it clicked open and closed
attaching my belongings
to the secure raft.

I loved how it opened a door
into the underbelly of the wide river
how it opened a window
in the rock of the Canyon's world.

The crew had set up the kitchen as soon as we got into camp. Hank hollered out "hot soup" and his voice rang up the canyon where we bathed. The sun disappeared and liqueur-colored light brushed the highest cliffs along the rim as we walked back. Though I wore nylon shorts and a light top, I was too warm. The sand, holding on to the heat of the day, reflected it back.

Tomato vegetable soup, crackers, and cheese, served as appetizers.

"I'm not very hungry," I said to Angie as we held our plates in line.

"Are you feeling weak and wobbly like me?" she asked.

"Yes. Unbalanced," I answered. "Walking the Bright Angel's part of it, missing John's part of it, not knowing who or where I am is the rest of it."

Supper menu: grilled steaks, a large salad, mashed potatoes, canned peas, and a Dutch-oven white cake baked to celebrate Nick's birthday. We washed our own dishes, first scrubbing our plates and forks in hot sudsy water, rinsing in hot water, then rinsing again in cool water with bleach added as a disinfectant.

By the campfire, Nick's wife, Suzanne, read him a poem she'd written for his birthday present. Then, Robb read hilarious narrative poems by David Lee. People clustered in groups to visit. Tired, my hips, calves, ankles, and feet sore, I told Angie good night and climbed to my solitary camp.

Undressing, I found the damp panties wadded in my pocket. I shook them out and hung them on a tamarisk branch to dry. Images of red racers and rattlesnakes, red ants and scorpions, flitted through my mind as I smoothed a place in the sand to unroll my bed in the last light. I whispered a prayer beneath the tamarisk tree that sheltered my spot and my imagined fears disappeared. I knew no harm would come to me.

Stretching out beneath the cliff-edged sky, I closed my eyes. The stars seduced them open again. Clouds gathered above the rim and I watched them roll in. It was so warm I left my sleeping bag open and laid there in a long T-shirt, my arms and legs bare. The slightest of breezes whispered up from the river.

I could not get comfortable. Two men snored, one above me on the hill, and one below me near the trees. But, there were other voices in the night, old ones, ones I'd heard before. They were calm and reverent, full of the night and their own well-kept secrets.

I could not sleep. I was not restless, but wakeful and aching, waiting for the lover that the river had hinted would come. Somewhere in the brush I heard the soft pad of animal feet, then the swish of a wing. I turned my head to see something flying right at me. I raised my arm and exhaled a slight hiss, and it bent away, wings sighing. I heard the sharp squeak of foraging bats, chirping crickets, the melodic song of the river. I dug out my foam earplugs, twisted them in my ears, and slept.

Sometime between midnight and morning, I woke and wandered through camp to find the stainless steel groover. Following the path with my small flashlight was difficult, but I discovered it nestled in a ring of stones up high above the river. Stars had once again replaced the clouds. Earlier the moon had risen and set in its half-full phase. So quiet, the river's sound echoed that of individual voices chanting the same song.

Back at my bedroll, I slipped a long-sleeved shirt over my shoulders, lay down, and studied the shooting stars slicing through the sky. The first one I wished on for John tending his cattle and helping hunters find elk. The second one I wished on for my mother alone in her home in Woodland Park.

"Dad," I whispered, "what do you think about me being here in the desert on the banks of a big river?"

My Father's Pillow

I squished it down really small and
squeezed it in my already stuffed duffle.

It rode in the plane's belly,
on the back of a burro,
until it was re-stuffed into a dry sack
and bounced around all day on a boat.

Tossed and thrown
by strange hands on bag lines,
it was carried up and down sandy hills
to a secluded camp site
where I took it out,
fluffed it, shook off the sand,
propped it on my life jacket.

Settling my head in its softness,
gazing at uncountable stars,
I tried to guess which one
was Dad's indomitable spirit shining.

Below Elves' Chasm

At daylight, I shook the sand off my sleeping bag and rolled it, folded my pair of tree-dried panties and tucked them into the bottom of my clothes bag along with the other pairs I'd foolishly brought.

Between the first call for coffee and breakfast, the boatmen packed their gear, stowed it, and made the boats ready for the big bags of tents and the smaller bags full of sleeping kits and personal gear.

The crew worked in harmony and the guests pitched in, shuffling dry bags onto the boats. Without experience to know how to assist, and not wanting to get in the way, I stayed apart, watching from the hill, observing, absorbing, and writing.

Breakfast menu: fresh fruit, cream of wheat, strawberries, yogurt, sausage, fried potatoes, French toast with syrup.

While we sat in the sand to eat, Robb forewarned us, "We're going to hit some major rapids today. All the gems: Crystal, Agate, Sapphire, Turquoise, Ruby, and Serpentine. Better dress warm."

I wore my splash gear to stay drier on the boat. The purple jacket and yellow pants caused Lana to say, "You look like a coral reef fish."

"It's okay," I laughed. "If I fall overboard, they'll be able to find me."

Riding in the back of Stefan's boat with Gina, the gem rapids splashed past one right after the other in a colorful disarray of water, spray, and foam. Small talk, Gina's warm, accepting smile, and Stefan's easygoing attitude helped me relax.

The tension blocking circuits from poetic reverie to pen in hand eased, so I pulled out my Rite in the Rain waterproof notebook and wrote: "Powell Plateau divides the landscape. Sheer red rock walls slide down to emerald water where a sloping dune with chiseled edge carved by lapping waves is graced with green-lace tamarisk that drifts like smoke over gray boulders. A heron hangs suspended above a wide shelf before settling his wings in a statue-like stance. Dragonflies dance rapid above the river. I don't feel small here. I've heard people say they feel dwarfed by the magnificence and magnitude of the landscape, that they are infinitesimal compared to the Canyon, but this river enlarges my heart, broadens my perspective, makes me big enough to embrace centuries of wildness and weather that coalesced to form this wonder."

Leaning back, I looked all around me, then wrote: "The river has sheared the sides off the cliffs leaving smooth, white pearly lines. The glistening face of rock shined by eons of polishing wind and water. Rock sculpted like pottery in shades of pink and gray, the silver sheen on schist, fluted like carved crystal, gargoyle shapes, gypsy designs. Very high up where red cliffs are layered like baklava, a bird chirps. Barrel cactus bend into the light. They lean toward warmth and sun. The sand is taupe and pinkish beige tinged with the sparkle of stars, a line of wet silver at water's edge. Tall grass, thick onshore, weaves a yellow, gray, green tapestry of tassels that tremble like wheat above calm water. A black rock, half out of the water, rises like a whale's back. The far-off roar of a rapid we've passed sounds like silence expressed."

I looked up to see Gina writing also.

"Why do words seem so wonderful when we're jotting them on the page, and then seem so horrid when we go back and reread?" I asked.

"Don't know," she said. "But it's true. Perhaps the secret is to not go back and reread. Self-editing is the enemy of inspiration."

"Angie told me you lost your father not long ago," I said.

"Yes, about a year and a half," she said.

"It's hard, isn't it? Mine's been gone almost three. I wonder if I'll ever adjust."

"Probably not," she said. "We don't ever really get over losing someone we love. Were you and your father close?"

"The last few years. We managed to call a truce and agree to accept one another for who we were, but before that it was touch and go. He was a tough dad, military-minded, always right with a tendency to be critical. He harbored a terrible temper, yet he was generous and caring too. We knew he loved us even when he was pitching a fit."

"Mine was my best friend. When I lost him, I lost part of myself," Gina said.

We lay back and watched the sun and sky go by, the canyon walls replete with colors and textures, great blue herons on rocks and in flight above the water, a small flock of birds with rapid wing beats whistling by.

"Stefan," I said, tapping our boatman on the shoulder.

"Hmm?" he replied, stretched out almost horizontal, the oars loose in his hands.

"Your laid-back manner softens me, opens my mind and allows the Canyon full access."

He grinned. "In high school, everyone called me by my last name, Greiner. Before freshman year was out they had nicknamed me Greiner the Recliner."

We laughed and I wrote: "He leans back on his bedroll,

an amused expression on his face and something certain tells me that Stefan's in his rightful place."

We floated, luxuriating in warmth during a calm stretch of water. I went on writing: "A breeze brushes bare legs beginning to speckle in the sun. The landscape is unreal and dreamlike, rosy cake rock with creamy frosting, brownie crust on top of the cliffs, the shades pink icing mottled like marble. Tracks in the sand are written messages I can't read. Dark green datura, rich as velvet cloth, mixes with bright green creeper that crawls across the sand. Buzzing insects, cicadas maybe, call from both sides of the Canyon. Sometimes the river smells glassy and sharp. It reflects back a placid jade face. Wind and rapid roar compete for space in my ears as the river vees into a fast-moving chute."

"Laurie," Gina warned. I glanced up from scribbling, stuffed the notebook and pen into the front zip pocket of my splash jacket, closed the Velcro throat opening, and grabbed on to a black strap. I smiled at Gina and she smiled back. We were in our element too, the world of excitement, sensory experience, images, and yet-unwritten words.

On our lunch stop, Robb guided us up Shinumo Creek to a waterfall. The spill of fancy-dancing water called me. Leaving my camera and fanny pack on a flat rock, I searched for Robb and found him squatting in the shadow of a wall near the falls.

"Would you please hold these for me?" I asked, handing him my sunglasses.

"Sure thing," he said.

I dove into the clear pool and swam, submerging myself in the pounding water. Cold, hard pellets beat my head, neck, and shoulders. It was a natural, no-expense massage. Nick waved at me and I followed him into the cavernous room behind the falls where the water was waist-deep.

Swimming out beneath the spray, I splashed again and again like a willful child. My lipstick floated out of my pocket, but Suzanne captured it for me before it disappeared downstream.

Standing thigh-deep to catch my breath, I searched for the new penny John had given me for good luck, but it was no longer in the tiny Velcro-closed watch pocket of my shorts. Uneasiness gripped my stomach. The penny represented my one connection to John in the Canyon. I couldn't believe I'd lost it already.

I shrugged off the glimmer of guilt. If it had to be lost and end up someplace, then the bottom of the pool where I took my first swim was as good a place as any.

I dried off in the sun. Then, sitting alone by the river, I ate a sandwich. Small brown butterflies, darting like hummingbirds from grass stem to grass stem, provided my entertainment.

Hummingbird in August

See how she dips the tip of her tongue
into the dark blue delphinium,
all buzz and hum, dart and drift,
her legs tucked up under a pale green body,
soft and tender as new leaves.

She hovers just inches from my eyes
where I wait on the step to see her sip
her breakfast, hear her wing beats
change pitch as she picks the flower
that will serve up the most sweetness.

Barely breathing, I blink.
She swivels and stares in the cool air
appraising the bill of my ball cap,
her tail shifting to keep her still
until I purse my lips and she disappears.

The afternoon drifted by. Not as big as the gems of the morning, the rapids—110 Mile, Hakatai, and Waltenberg— had three to eight-foot drops. Some great power sapped my energy and I wondered how to recharge my batteries. No one spoke. Gina, stretched out, her cap off, looking like a contented colt, chestnut mane sparkling in the sun. I leaned back against some dry bags and wrote: "Limestone created by the ocean, travertine, schist, and sandstone, a cave carved in granite. Bright Angel shale cream colored gold. Glare and shadow, shades of gray and pink, rocks dripping, black and green in muted light. A lone fly hitches a ride, dashing here and there, landing on shoulders and caps. The oar locks rock and click. A hussy-bold breeze demands attention."

Stopping at Elves' Chasm, we followed Robb on a hard climb up a side canyon with gigantic boulders, a plummeting stream, and monkey flowers carmine bright against emerald leaves. I tested out my Tevas, the spider-like tread giving me a good grip on the boulder-to-boulder trail. Weak and shaky, I sat and watched others climb into the rock grotto and emerge in the heart of the waterfall.

Standing splay-legged on the ledge, they jumped into an azure pool. Lana leapt, then Angie, then Lana again. I snapped pictures of them in the air, arms up and legs askew. Robb and half a dozen others made the leap and splashed down, disappearing for seconds until they reemerged swimming for the sandbar. On the verge of tears, I sought a quiet spot to offer prayers to the Mother of Waters.

As I made my way back down to the river ahead of the crowd, I encountered Nick sprawled on the rocks, his face eye-level with a monkey flower. Walking on, I composed the image in my mind: "A man from Massachusetts lies belly down on a long flat rock and tilts a tiny tripod toward the stream, angling his large lens, squirming forward to catch just the right light to photograph one bright blossom. The delicate bloom, red as new-painted lips, trembles near rushing water."

Stefan pulled our boat onto a beach to collect firewood. Daniel, who had joined us after lunch and ridden in front all afternoon, jumped out to tie the boat. Then, he and Stefan gathered long pieces of driftwood. Daniel passed back a bucket full of branches.

"Look at the intricate designs on each stick," I said to Gina. "Each branch believed it was lost in the river's rushing water. Each was remade a creation shaped by water and wind, sand and sun, and forgot that it was once a tree. Each washed up on the white beach to bleach away its wet darkness, until human hands found it and turned it into fire."

"That's profound," she said. "Hurry, write it down."

"Tell me what I said," I laughed.

Floating again, I tapped Gina on the shoulder and pointed out a gigantic dead tree stuck up high in the rocks.

"It must be thirty feet above the river," I said.

"That shows the kind of floods there were in the Canyon before modern engineers constructed dams," she said.

The image impressed me and I stared at that tree skeleton until it grew smaller and smaller, then disappeared from sight. The lives of trees, like our own, end in different ways, at different times. We never know what will make them fall.

The Passing of a Ponderosa

The morning was silent except
for a fly that followed me
up the forest trail, buzzing
a last serenade of the season.
Rain-wet plants exhaled
as I crushed them underfoot
into the soft, dark earth.
Slowly, far away,
a huge sigh of giving up,
a sharp hard crack like a rifle,
then a loud long crash
like reverberating thunder.

The hush that answered
was palpable as prayer,
and I heard the hum of bees
exiting a nearby aspen,
a few warning notes
from a mourning dove,
the chastising chatter of a squirrel.

What wrenched giant roots
from side hill soil?
One robin resting on a bald spire,
an unexpected breeze,
the weight of one raindrop
falling from branch to barren branch?

Night came to the Canyon as we pulled into camp, dusk settling on the sandy shoulders of the river like a shawl woven of stars. The other boats were already moored. People bustled about setting up the kitchen and finding campsites.

"Thank you, Stefan," Gina said as we climbed from the boat, "for such a good time."

She patted him on the back. Tears seeped into her eyes.

I squeezed Gina's hand as we walked away. "I know," I said. "I wish I could cry against his shoulder for giving us such a beautiful day."

Stefan's Skin

gleams copper rich, new penny bright in the sun
not as red-gold as my sorrel gelding
not as deep brown as a bull elk
but something as rich and warm as devil's food
　　dessert.

He rows with rhythm
canting his body back and forth
each power stroke destined
to move the boat forward through calm water.

Dark beige striations along his shoulders
tighten and stretch when his muscles move.
A round puckered scar beneath one blade
looks like an old bullet hole or an arrow wound.

He seems such a gentle soul, more Zen
or zephyr than renegade or marauding warrior,
his oriental eyes soft and wise. Still, here on the river,
my imagination runs loose and wild.

As I shuffled up a steep sandy hill to look for a camp spot, Daniel, who had slept below me last night, was coming down.

"Hi," I said. "Sorry to mention this, but do you know you snore?"

"Yeah. Did I keep you awake?"

I smiled back. "No offense. I just need a quiet place to sleep."

"Come on," he said, taking my dry bag to carry.

"Here's my spot," he indicated his camp setup, "but come look at this."

We climbed. "The Penthouse," he said. "Just the spot for a light sleeper."

A flat, lightly graveled spot rested high above the camp under the face of sheer cliffs with a grassy area under a tree and a small cactus outcropping surrounded by big boulders.

"Oh, this is perfect," I said. "Thank you."

"I'll go get your tent bag for you," he said, sprinting down the hill.

The cliffs glowed red in the late light. I loved my sanctuary and loved Daniel for leading me to it. I stood a long time, looking upriver, high enough to see the top of the canyon walls' color striations, jade water, rose-beige sand, moss-green brush, black schist, jumbled gray boulders, layers of multicolored sandstone shining beige, red, cream, ochre and brown with grayish white spots, the very top layer a pinkish brown with mottled red changing from darker to lighter shades. I spotted Angie, Helen, Lana, and Gina on a sandy spit by a group of tall trees.

Far away from everyone and everything, I relaxed, humming as I draped wet clothes on low branches, placed my sleep pad on the fine gravel in a tiny wash, unrolled my sleeping bag and hung my glasses and cap on a dead branch for safekeeping.

Gina appeared, breathless and laughing, lugging my tent bag.

"Goodness. Daniel told me where you were. You pick the oddest places to camp. Do you want to go and wash?" she asked.

"Sure," I said, and we walked down to the river, followed the path past the groover and took the signal cushion so no one would bother us.

On a long smooth beach with calm water, we stripped, scrubbed ourselves with suds and silt-laden water to get the sweat rinsed off. I put on a long, lightweight patterned shift and felt clean and renewed with my wet hair down around my shoulders drying in the breeze.

As night cook, Stefan fixed Cajun fried catfish, salad, rice, and sautéed zucchini for supper. Everyone gathered around the grill-contained campfire to eat, a cozy setting with bits and scraps of conversation floating past. Gina and I sat together chatting about writing. I gathered our empty plates, plus a dozen more. As I scrubbed dishes, Robb joined me to rinse and stack.

"Tell me about you," I said.

"Oh, there's not much to know. I'm on the river most of the year. When I'm off I join my wife at the North Rim."

"Does that work out? All the time being apart?" I asked.

"Seems to work for us," he said. "Besides, you know what they call a boatman without a wife or a girlfriend?"

"No, what?" I replied.

"Homeless," he said, his accompanying offbeat laugh quite captivating.

"I wonder what you'd call a ranch wife without a rancher," I said.

We wandered back to the fire where Helen, Lana, Gina and Angie were taking turns massaging each other's sore calves. Remembering my promise to give Lana and Gina each a foot rub, I joined in. Caleb slipped into the group with some Irish sipping whiskey.

"Anyone need a medicinal nip?" he asked.

"Will it help a scratchy throat?" I asked.

"Absolutely," he replied.

I took a tiny swallow, felt it burn its way down. Then, passed the bottle to Lana next to me. As the campfire burned down to embers, the laughter and conversation softened. Robb sat with his back against a smooth oblong board, a piece of driftwood that looked like the keel off of someone's boat.

"Want to hear a poem?" he asked.

"Yes," we answered in union.

He recited a funny narrative about a hog farmer's trip into town.

"Laurie," Angie said, "you recite one for us."

"The only thing I know by heart is 'Wenn Ich Ein Voglein War.' A piece we had to memorize in high school German class."

"That'll do," Robb said.

I took a long breath, closed my eyes, and recited the poem with all the fervor the setting called for. Caleb spoke to me in German, but I pretended I didn't hear. If I'd known he spoke the language, I would never have been brave enough to recite such romantic verse.

The soreness at the back of my throat tightened and dried.

"I'm tired and achy," I said to Gina. "I need to go to bed."

She walked me to my camp, showing the way with her

93

flashlight, and hugged me good night. I wiggled into my sleeping bag, but had to get up to pee. I didn't want to dress and traipse down to the river in the dark, so I turned an empty water bottle into a tiny chamber pot.

The wind kicked up and heat lightning capered between the clouds. A drop of rain bounced off my cheek. I worried for awhile that it might storm. Night sounds serenaded me. Crickets called in symphonic harmony with the roar of the river until I fell asleep.

A loud crack, sounding like the earth had opened to engulf me, startled me awake, my heart sprinting. I wanted to get up and walk around, ease the restlessness, but I was too tired. Lying there, thinking of John, I said into the darkness, "How are you? I miss you. Do you believe I love you? Do dreams disturb or bless your sleep?"

Elves' Chasm

Years from now I see myself coming back
my body small and shrunken
long gray braids brushing my waist
making my way up the steep side canyon
placing each bare foot with caution on the slick rock
pausing to kneel and touch the blood-red funny faces
of the seep-spring monkey flowers that grow
wild in the stream's cool spray and shade.

I'll swim across the unruffled face of the blue pool
climb up slippery rocks past maidenhair fern
and deep green moss into the dark grotto
where water reaches out and falls with the force
of a million summer rains and winter snows.

I'll wait on the ledge bathed in mist and sunlight
and listen for his voice calling to me: "Jump!"
Then I'll leap, arms flung wide to embrace the day,
toes pointed to push apart the water, which surrounds
me like cool silk sheets in the darkest of nights.

When my face finds the surface and I breathe in
a gasping rush of air, I'll find him there
waiting to wrap me in a towel of warm wonder.

Below Bedrock Canyon

Before first light, I woke to high-pitched keening sounds, voices that didn't seem human, or animal either, just something deep from the soul of the earth. I waited, holding my breath, listening, but nothing happened. Again I lay awake, thinking about my first days on the river. It was difficult for me. Struggling to maintain my balance in an environment where I felt clumsy and awkward, I was forever tripping or stumbling, just barely catching myself before I crashed and fell. I needed to pay attention, to concentrate, to learn every lesson that came my way.

In the midst of wanting to be wiser and stronger, I had the strangest desire to die. It was more than a yearning to be left behind on a beach so I could be alone, or a longing to be one with the Canyon, to let my blood and bones go back to the earth where I belonged. It was an overpowering energy that rushed at me in bright guise and said, "It's just one small step," when I was standing on the lip of a cliff way above the water, or, "Just let go," when we were in the white, cold, wet heart of a rapid.

The notion of falling or of drowning was not a dark thought. It did not frighten me. Rather, it was lovely, a thought full of transcendent light, as if in the middle of a long fall I'd sprout wings and fly, or finding myself stuck beneath the weight of water I'd grow fins and swim.

Bizarre wishes, they didn't seem to be so much about dying as about aching for an otherness, of being something different than what I was. Not something human and awkward, ungainly and ugly, but something as rare and fine and at home in its environment as the bighorn ram perched on a narrow rock ledge browsing brush.

I wondered what it would be like to hike up a side canyon, take off my pack, leave my water bottles and boots, socks, shirt and shorts, even my bandanna, and just keep walking into the light and shadows until I could no longer move. What would it be like to take off trusty seventy-seven, clip it to a black strap so the wind wouldn't steal it, then tip off the back of the boat and disappear? What if, when I closed my eyes at night under a sky full of irresistible stars, I decided to just keep on sleeping, not waking up when Hank hollered "Hot coffee?"

When a hint of light burnished the sky, I rose to talk with the rocks and offer a prayer to the tree that sheltered me while I slept. Then, I walked to the river to wash my face and empty my chamber pot.

Hank was already in the kitchen, frying bacon, potatoes, and eggs, making oatmeal, and setting out granola with brown sugar and raisins. I snitched a piece of banana from a bowl brimming also with cantaloupe, honeydew melon, and Granny Smith apples.

"Hank," I said, "can I have some salt?"

"Sure, what for? I mean how much?" he asked.

"Just a teaspoon, to gargle with. My throat's sore."

"You want some whiskey and lemon?"

"No," I laughed. "Not this early."

"You got a cold?" he asked.

"Don't think so. Maybe an allergy of some kind."

"That happens here sometimes. Lots of different trees, the dry air."

"Can I have one of these?" I asked, holding up an orange.

"Sure, honey, you can have anything you want," he said, then turned and hollered "Breakfast" at the top of his lungs.

Winter Fruit

"Love flares across a bowl of oranges,"
writes Alfred Corn in his poem
"Notes from a Child of Paradise,"
and perhaps it might just be true.
A woman told me the other day
she smells oranges before the first blinding
slash of a migraine cuts across her eyes.
But, for me, oranges mean a headache of the heart,
my first so long ago I barely remember
the downtown Chicago apartment or the man
who gave my girlfriend a bowl of yogurt and oranges
in the cold December dawn of their morning-after,
while I shuddered as she chewed tangy chunks,
licking white cream from her lips like a spoiled cat.

Not long after, marooned on a winter island
in the far north with a man I'd just met,
I opened the door that no one ever knocked on
to find a stranger holding snowshoes and a sack of
    oranges,
his beard rimmed with white frost, his eyes startled
with the surprise of finding a woman in his friend's
    cabin.
For the days he stayed, we ate oranges like savages
each bitter dawn, and I wondered which man I loved,
the one who devoured me every night,
or the one who ate me with his eyes during the day.

Over many years, season after season, I seldom bought
oranges at the store. I settled instead for apples
and bananas, though I once picked up an orange to feel
its weight, as round and firm as my own breast.
My tongue tightened and tingled. My mouth went wet,
as I placed the cool orb back in its bin and walked on.

Then, this December, a California friend sent a
    carton
of oranges which I found sitting in snow at the gate.
All fall I had been brittle and dry, the juice gone
from my kisses as life pulled my husband and me
in different directions, so different that he chose
an orange one morning, peeled it precisely with a
    spoon
and took the whole glistening globe into another
    room to eat,
while I carefully cut mine into eight even slices,
tore out the pith with my teeth, swallowed the gold
    juice
and left the yellow-orange smiles on the white
    counter,
the fragrance coloring the kitchen long into the night.

The following day, I left, flying across the country
to hold winter in another way for a week.
When I returned he said he ate an orange every morning
and crossed white-out days one by one off the calendar;
his eyes smoldered as I skinned the peel from four
    oranges,
sectioned them, sliced them into small perfect pieces,
stirred them with powdered sugar, coconut and
    pecans.

100

While the wind raged, we sat in front of the fire
eating ambrosia; for days after, snowbound,
I smelled oranges in the air, tasted oranges on his lips.

I gobbled down orange sections as I hurried to pack up my camp. No time to write. Everyone was hauling their gear to the beach and forming lines to pass the dry bags and sleeping pads onto the boats. Robb hollered, "Last call for the potty!" Then, he collected the groover and stowed it on board Meg's baggage boat. When we pulled away from camp the only things left behind were footprints in the sand and the smoothed-down spots where we had made our beds.

The day quieted as we took off from the boat beach with Lana and me riding in the back of Robb's boat. On the long stretch of flat water, no sound intruded except the river and the oars. The kayaks floated past, all different colors, Caleb's a dark blue. He lifted his paddle in a casual salute, and Lana and I waved back.

Drifting along the silk-smooth surface, only a few mild rapids interrupted my daydreaming until we pulled into shore. Robb nudged us along a trace through Blacktail Canyon where the sidewalls, stained dark, reached up hundreds of feet to reveal a slice of sky. The sun blazed outside, but inside was dim, cool, and hushed. Rock walls tumbled into a jumble of stones and boulders, and a rill murmured along the center of the floor.

Robb talked geology: "This is schist, a foliated, metamorphic rock. Two billion years ago this was ocean floor with sediments and lava flows. Then the earth's plates, sliding together, caused gigantic pressure and the quartz melted out, the magma squeezed up. Billions of years ago there was granite intrusion underneath the continent. Part of the Grand Canyon super group. An area stretched out and slid and tilted with basin in between. This became the dawning edge of the Cambrian sea, the Great Unconformity."

The geology discourse eluded me, but I loved listening

to Robb's voice, enjoyed trying to fit the strange words together like a crossword puzzle. A raven's caw echoed up high near the sliver of silver sky and my attention shifted to its gliding flight.

Daniel hiked farther up the canyon and I followed. Stagnant pools watered small trees and other vegetation trying to grow up through the rock. Scrambling for footing, sticking to the hard surfaces to avoid leaving footprints in the undisturbed mud, I reached for boulders that were rough-textured, a sensation like an elephant's skin beneath my hands.

At the dead end, Daniel squatted against the wall, craning his neck to look at the distant ceiling where water fell in a miniature cascade. The stone behind the waterfall was chalk-white and slick with moss and algae.

"Beautiful, isn't it?" he asked.

"Yes," I said. "Deserving of an offering or at least a prayer."

He looked like he didn't know what to say.

"Do you hear that?" I asked.

"No," he said. "What?"

"The weeping."

"I don't hear anything except the drip of water," he said.

"Probably my imagination," I said, the sound making my skin prickle.

I swirled my fingers in the glassy pool and touched the moisture to my forehead before walking back through thick shadows and into sunlight.

Blacktail Canyon

Somewhere in the dark heart of this narrow place
there is a spirit who mourns the lost sunlight.

I hear her sigh. I feel her searching for
the soul of day in the dank coolness.

She is used to silence. My footsteps disturb
her sleep and she yawns, rising to walk beside me.

I touch her cold shoulder and she shivers.
I listen while she weeps as a widow weeps.

When I walk back into the morning sun,
she stays behind, blinking and afraid.

We headed on down the river and beached the boats once more on a sandy bar with an extreme rise above slow water. The crew set up the lunch table on a high spot in some patches of tamarisk shade.

Angie, Lana, Helen, and Gina followed Suzanne and Nick's example and washed their hair. Serving as hand-maiden, I squirted soap on their wet heads and as they scrubbed I poured cups of river water over them.

"Ouch," Angie laughed. "It's giving me an ice cream headache."

The muddy clay bottom of the river sucked at our sandaled feet. We slogged like a bunch of drunken sailors, holding on to each other, listing first left, then right, making our way back to dry ground.

I made myself a sandwich and squatted in the sun to eat. Robb, clowning around, performed a series of rapid-fire somersaults down the sandy slope and splashed into the river. Meg mimicked him, rolling over and over like a large round rock, and catapulted into the water.

"Lunchtime entertainment," Hank said, sitting down next to me.

"It's fun to watch them play, isn't it?"

"Got to make time for fun or life's just not worth it," he said.

"Truer words were never spoken," I said. "We should allow ourselves to goof around once in awhile."

"Load up," Robb called out.

Hank smiled at me and jumped up to help the rest of the crew.

I stood and watched the water running past.

"Laurie?" Lana said, walking up. "Are you okay? You look sad."

"No," I said. "Not really sad. I'm lonely. I miss John so

105

much. I just wish he were here to hold me for a little while."

"I can do that for you," she said, and put her arms around me.

We stood embraced on the beach until it was time to go.

I had tears in my eyes when I walked back to Robb's boat where Meg and Hank stood watching.

"Is everything all right?" Hank asked.

"Oh," I said, "I'm just homesick."

"Ah," Meg sighed.

"Well," Hank replied, "I'll hug you too if it'll help any."

I went right into his arms, into a big, strong, hearty bear hug. His whiskers rubbed soft on my cheek and he smelled like sun and sand, the river and wind.

"Thank you, Hank," I said.

"My pleasure, whenever you like," he replied.

Lana and I, Suzanne, Nick, and Daniel rode with Robb in the afternoon. Daniel and I traded spots back and forth to rest our backs because the one who sat far in the front had nothing to lean against. Larger and more dangerous, the rapids kept us hunkered down and holding on. Lana chattered with nervous excitement.

"Aren't you scared?" she asked.

"No," I answered, "I trust Robb to keep us safe."

Robb snorted and said, "Haven't you learned yet not to trust men?"

"Touché," I replied.

Of all the day's rapids, Specter grabbed my attention. The left side of the river curved into a narrow chute and the right side swept around a giant boulder. Robb rowed hard to get the boat in the best position. I turned and glimpsed his apprehension. My palms oozed sweat at that expression. He made everything seem so simple even when it wasn't. I mouthed a prayer that his knowledge and skill and love of the river would give us safe passage.

I squeezed my eyes shut, but the image remained: ghost-like white water, shapes and visions dancing as we rushed toward the wall of rock battered by waves. In Robb's face, a strange tension caught and tamed. I glanced around to find his face dripping, the grimace transformed to a grin, his eyes burning fire-bright as the apparition faded.

Watching Robb ease us into more gentle water, I thought back over the past few days, and realized that my eyes always sought and found him in the crowd. Or from far away I'd hear his strange, distinctive laugh and smile. The attraction didn't delve romantic or sexual notions; it garnered respect and curiosity. I admired him and yearned to emulate him. He exhibited the traits of a keen observer, not only of the Canyon and the river, but also of all of us in his care. Calm and quiet, he appeared everywhere at once, checking on things, going about the endless chores around camp. Though honored as trip leader, he pitched in with every facet of camp life: he cooked and washed dishes, moved the groover, loaded and unloaded gear, built fires, helped set up the kitchen and took it down again. Yet, he never appeared hurried or rushed. Taking things in stride, he remained patient and kind, spending time with each person in camp. Attentive to everyone's needs, he seemed to know before anyone asked what was wanted. No matter what happened in camp or on the river, Robb knew. He kept an eye on his boatmen, making certain each raft came through every rapid, standing on his boat looking back up the river until the last boatman arrived in camp. One of the first ones up, he was usually the last to go to bed.

He handled complaints without being upset and listened to compliments with shy appreciation. He never spoke an unkind word. If the crew goofed around when there was work to do, he never said a thing, he simply worked twice as hard himself until they took notice and pitched in. Sharing an easy camaraderie with the men, he offered his knowledge of the river and the Canyon openly. Sensitive and conciliatory with the women, he offered a sympathetic ear and a tender touch. Never playing favorites, he found ways to be magnanimous to each of us.

"Robb?" I said, turning around to face him.

"Hmmm?"

"You're quiet."

"Uh-huh. I like to hear the river."

"Everyone's chatter too much?"

"Sometimes. But I like listening to stories too."

"With all the great things there are about being a boatman, what's the biggest drawback to your job?"

"Having to talk so much," he grinned, but I ignored his hint to hush.

"Is that why you go off by yourself at times?"

"Sure, it's my way to recharge. Plus, I like watching things from a distance, assess what's going on," he said.

"Sometimes you just disappear. I look around and you're gone. Then I look again, and you're back."

"Yep," he said.

"Is it magic? Are you some kind of a wizard?" I asked.

He laughed so hard, Lana stopped talking to Daniel, and said, "Okay, you two, what are you up to?"

"Nothing," I said.

"She's trying to make me blush," Robb said, laughing again.

"I am not," I said, waving my arm in a gesture of dismissal as I turned back around.

"Doing better?" Lana asked.

"Yes. I feel content and peaceful when I'm with Robb,"

I whispered. "Do you feel it too? That radiating calm, like a cat curled by a fire, all warm and relaxed."

"Of course," Lana whispered back. "He's wonderful. Magic."

"That's what I said," I giggled.

"Okay, you girls," Robb warned, "no secrets."

"Or, at least, let me in on it," Daniel said.

Lana and I tucked our heads in tighter.

"I admire him," I said, "his connection to the Canyon, his affinity for wildness, this love affair he has with the river."

"He's smart," Lana added. "Look at everything he tells us about astronomy, geology, and biology, the environment."

"Don't you think part of it is his reverence for indigenous people? He's so respectful."

"You know what I like," Lana said. "He likes to challenge himself, push himself. Test his mental acuity, his physical agility. And, he likes to play, mess around. Did you see him with Meg this morning?"

"I did," I said, smiling. "Lana, this might sound funny, but I admire him because he's so comfortable in his skin, so alive in every moment."

"Heads up," Robb warned.

With a now automatic response, Lana and I grabbed hold of our straps. Drenched by an onslaught of huge waves, we screamed together.

"That's what you get for gossiping," Robb laughed.

We pulled in to hike up a cliff face to visit an Anasazi ruin. The difficult climb meant moving slow, rock-to-rock, boulder-to-boulder, avoiding the spines on barrel cactus, trying to stay on the narrow trail as Robb advised.

Nestled under an overhanging cliff, the structure had been constructed of a series of flat red rocks.

"The site is sacred," Robb said. "Please don't bother anything. Don't pick up flint chips or pottery shards. This is one of only a few places where humans could get in or out of the Canyon from the rim by traveling along a tapered fault line in the rock," Robb said, moving closer.

A collection of flint and pottery pieces glistened on a big rock at the opening to the ruins. Robb's silence told us what he thought about the violation of etiquette.

"Well," he said, "since someone else set this up, let's talk about the kinds of pottery the ancestors of the Hopi created."

I drifted off to be by myself. The view, long and full, was unequaled from the high point. A raven wafted past, cocking its head to look at the people clustered against the cliff. A feather floated free from its wing, twisting down in slow motion to settle just a few feet away. I picked it up, felt the barbules through my fingers.

I waited in the shadows until the others began the long hike back down the hill. Then, kneeling, I placed the feather as a prayer offering in the center of the ruins. Standing a moment longer, I placed my hands flat against the back wall to feel the memories of the old ones who had lived there.

When I turned the first switchback going down the trail, Robb leaned there against a boulder, waiting.

"Okay?" he asked.

"I wish I lived here," I said.

He nodded, and made way for me to pass. All the way back to the boats, I heard the sound of his steps on the stones behind me.

Anasazi Site

Here in the bright noonday sun
red ruins made of flat rocks
shine like old dried blood
against the heart of a high cliff.

The walls speak to the water far below:
I have not forgotten how you felt
rubbing against my rough skin,
how we made another world
by being washed and worn together.

We camped early in a rocky, brushy spot with cactus all around and the access to the river difficult. The long, narrow stretch of beach interspersed with many trees didn't allow much room for campsites, so I tucked in tight on a flat with the other women.

"Welcome to Tent City," Angie said, hugging me.

Gina helped me set up my tent for the first time. The wind gusted without stopping and we scrambled to keep the nylon flies from disappearing upriver. I fussed about the cramped space. Surrounded by big rocks, Tent City's sandy spot became the avenue everyone traveled to go farther down the beach or up to the kitchen area. Shane hiked past, recruiting people.

"Want to climb up to the waterfall?" he called.

"Too tired," I yelled back as Helen and I stumbled through large cobbles to the river.

A black-and-white patterned snake halted us mid-step.

"Whoa," I said, watching its lithe body wind gracefully through the rocks. "What is it?"

"King snake?" Helen guessed. "It doesn't have any rattles. It must be four feet long. Should we tell Robb?"

"No," I said. "He's moving away from everyone. Let's leave him be."

Someone hollered, "Groover's too close to camp," and we laughed.

When I saw Robb moving the pot, I hurried to help carry the water buckets, foot pump, and soap used for cleaning hands. Along the edge of a dry wash, Robb set the groover on a giant flat stone under the shelter of a large tree. It looked like a primitive throne. He turned away from the river and pointed up the side canyon.

"One of my favorite views," he said.

Far up the wide gravel bed, late light shimmered gold

112

and mauve on the cliff face. In the split second of time that it took for us to both breathe, I recognized Robb as a true kindred spirit. Neither of us said a word. We stood there on the pebbled ground, side by side, inches apart, watching night come quiet to the river.

Tired of fussing over the organization of stuff in my tent, I joined the other women gathered for girl talk. Bunched up like broodmares, we shared secrets in the nippy breeze.

"Okay," Lana asked, "which guy would you choose if you could? I like Caleb."

Angie, hesitant, said, "Me too."

Gina refused to admit an attraction to anyone.

Deciding to be brave and join in the fun, I said, "I'd choose Robb."

Helen broke in laughing, saying, "I'm sorry, darling, but he's already taken. You take Daniel instead."

"Oh, Daniel, Daniel," I said. "Daniel seems like a little brother. He's very sweet and unassuming."

I pulled my gritty-with-sand, mostly melted lipstick out of my pocket and swiped it on my lips.

"Vanity strikes again," Lana said.

"Hey," I countered, "at least I left my blush, eye shadow, and mascara at home. I'd rather walk around without any clothes than without my lipstick."

"What color?" she asked, holding out her hand.

I gave her the tube, bracing myself for her reaction.

"Nearly nude. How funny," she said. "It's hard, isn't it, wanting to look beautiful when faced with wind-burnt skin and baggy, sleep-deprived eyes?"

I laughed and said, "I glanced in my tiny mirror this morning and gasped. I put that thing at the bottom of my dry bag. I won't look again."

113

All of us had serious cases of hat hair. I taught Gina how to wear her scarf on her forehead to keep her short coppery mane out of her eyes. Lana lost her hairbrush, so she borrowed Helen's. I broke the handle off my nylon-bristled brush and some of the teeth out of my comb trying to get the tangles out of my wind-blown hair, which was oily from sweating in the sun and brittle on the ends from river water. It was too cold to wash hair, so I braided mine into pigtails, and tied a bandanna on as a headband.

"Hey, Pocahontas," Lana said, "you look like you're about fourteen."

I found Hank working in the kitchen.

"Hi," I said. "Can I beg another substitute husband hug?"

He dried off his hands, said, "Sure thing, Little Missy," and lifted me right off the ground. Suspended between sand and sky by his affection, I said, "Hank, I'm going to come every morning and every night for one of your bear hugs."

"That's okay by me," he said, and went back to chopping cabbage.

While I filled my supper plate with spinach dip, crackers, cabbage slaw, smoked turkey, pasta, and green beans with water chestnuts in mushroom sauce, Robb sidled up and teased, "Ha, you look just like Heidi."

"Lana said Pocahontas," I laughed. "At least you don't think I look like Pollyanna."

I stood by the fire, savoring a piece of carrot cake. When Stefan walked up and tugged on one of my braids, I hugged him with my free arm and joked, "How did you make the cake so fast?"

"I used canned carrots," he whispered.

A small campfire spot above the beach beckoned and

everyone gathered. Robb played his harmonica as we sang "The Streets of Laredo" and "The Night Rider's Lament."

"Wish I'd brought my guitar," Angie said.

"Wish I had my fiddle," Caleb added.

"Suzanne," I asked, "what is the instrument you play just before bed, those high wailing notes that sound so wild and lonely? Is it some kind of a flute?"

"No, a chanter, the mouthpiece of the bagpipes," she answered. "I'm not bothering anyone, am I?"

"No," we said in unison.

"I love it," Angie said. "Your rendition of 'Amazing Grace' sounds perfect here in the Canyon."

Robb outlined tomorrow's hike: Seven miles up Tapeats Creek and down Deer Creek. Drawing a map in the sand, he showed us where we would leave the boats and where we would meet up with them again. At each spot on the trail where there was a creek, springs, or a waterfall, he dumped a stream of river water from a pot on the grill. Charming and entertaining, he made us laugh.

"Everyone pack a lunch at breakfast or you'll go hungry," he said.

"I don't think I can make that long a hike," I said to Lana and Angie.

"Me either," Gina said.

"Listen," Caleb said, "you don't want to miss this. The views are fantastic and Thunder River flows right out of the side of the cliff."

"I'm afraid I'll wimp out," I said.

"Nah. You can do it," he said.

"Will you walk behind me and prod me every time I want to quit?" I asked.

"Sure," he said. "And I'll cut a switch to use as a whip too."

He patted me on the shoulder, then reached over and squeezed Lana in a quick hug.

"Don't miss this," he said to her.

The moon's saffron light spilled around me as I squirmed into my sleeping bag positioned half in and half out of the tent. I woke to a light patter of rain on the fly. A blustery wind blew sand in my face until I tucked myself inside. Then, I could not sleep. Lines from Gerard Manley Hopkins's poems kept echoing in my brain. I turned on my flashlight and wrote them down, trying to piece together "The Windhover" and "God's Grandeur" from memory.

Next to me, Gina stirred, restless, not sleeping either.

"Gina," I whispered, "are you okay?"

"It's the river," she said. "The roaring keeps me awake."

"Do you want my other set of earplugs?" I asked. "Sometimes that works for me."

"Sure," she said. "Thanks."

Before dawn, I headed out in a misty rain to find the groover, but I could not follow the path with my tiny flashlight. Meg found me wandering in circles in the dark.

"Turn off the light and go by foot feel," she said and put me on the right trail.

In the dark, I sat on the cool throne with refreshing rain whispering down and wished I could see Robb's favorite view.

View of the World from the Bottom of a Gully

Slip-sliding down the steep side of a dry wash,
I walked where the elk walked,
crossing from sage flat to pine thicket,
from moonlit night to pink-streaked dawn,
from sleep and dreamless feeding into hiding,
when a glimpse of startling white
pierced the outside edge of my eye,
made me stop and turn in the very bottom
of the red earth's V to see a primrose blooming
among the gray-green brush and stumps
and stunted flood-warped trees.

From this funnel form threshold,
the sky was horizon-less with clouds caught
in a narrow slit of virgin blue that bends beyond
the chewed-off lip of earth high above my head.
Out of sight, ridges disappeared, whole mountain
ranges slid into the sea of what was not seen.
Fields and forests were forgotten.
The river ran only in echoed memory.
My feet began to root in that place,
push tough tendrils through my boots,
telling me to stay where the world disappeared.

Below Deer Creek Falls
at the Back-eddy

Shivering, I hustled to dress, pack my gear, and take down my tent. Hank cooked up pancakes and sausages, cream of wheat, granola, and fruit, while I prepared a peanut butter and peach jelly sandwich, and added an apple, an orange, granola bar, fig bars, and a package of M&M's to take with me. Since I was ready, I spent the early hour hauling gear to the beach while the others had breakfast and packed lunches.

Lana and I rode in Hank's boat for the short trip to a beach where we'd begin our hike. He wore his straw hat with a plastic covering to protect it from the misty drizzle.

"That's a neat deal," I said.

"Robb calls it 'the hat condom,' " Hank said. "But it works."

"Wish I had one for the hat I wear on the ranch," I said.

"I figured you for a ranch gal," he said. "Cattle and horses, right?"

"You got it. I bet you've been there and done that," I said.

"Sure have," he said.

Hank's left shoulder was tattooed with a trio of Native American pictographs. As he rowed, they moved and danced, coming alive in the dazzle of sunlight.

Out of the boats, we kept our river sandals on to cross a wide creek. Captivating yellow flowers brightened the brush on the other side.

"What are these?" I asked Robb. "They look like our Colorado evening primroses."

"Close," he said. *"Oenothera hookerii,* Hooker's evening primrose."

Sitting on a rock, I changed into my hiking boots and arranged my gear for the climb. A not-so-wild turkey sauntered up, going from person to person looking for handouts. Whenever someone rattled a paper, the turkey thought it meant lunch and rushed over. When he came to check me out, I took a photo of him just two feet away. Suzanne took out part of a sandwich to give him.

"No," I said, "don't feed him. He'll get spoiled. Then, what will he eat when we're gone?"

We watched as the big bird meandered off into the rocks.

Eating an Apple

Cast aside, sick of love, I comforted myself
one August evening by eating an apple.

I split the ripe fruit exactly in half
and revealed its inner star,
then cut it precisely into quarters,
carefully slicing away the core
with its still attached stick-like stem
and frowzy brown blossom end.

I took my first bite slowly,
studying the tough texture
of red peel against my teeth,
savoring the sweet-sharp juice
crushed from virgin pulp.

Chewing, thinking,
I considered the history and heritage
of little hard seeds sitting
in transparent cradles,
waiting for the soft pome to rot,
waiting for a return to earth.

Startled, seeing their inherent
desire to be trees, I carried the cuts
of withered core outside
and scattered them in tall grass
beneath a rain wet bush.

As I turned away, a bold magpie
settled on the wood rail of the deck.
Head nodding, tail bobbing,
he strutted his scavenger stuff
over to my offering and ate.

Robb crossed the creek carrying a cup of water. He wore knee-length shorts, a long-sleeved shirt, and black flip-flops. When the trail was easy Robb went barefoot, so I decided that the flip-flops meant the hike today would be a tough go. His medium-size fanny pack held a first aid kit and his lunch.

"All righty," he said, "ready for a little stroll."

I groaned and fell into line.

Daniel walked up behind me and said, "I've been on this hike before. They call it 'the death march.'"

"Great," I said, groaning again. "I'm glad it's cloudy and cool. If it had been hot, I doubt I would have had the courage to attempt the climb."

Starting up a steep, switchbacking, barely visible trail on the side of the cliff, Robb warned us that this first part of the journey was 2,000 feet straight up. His stroll was more like a forced military drill, so there was no time to stop for a breather, no time to pause and look around, no time to stop and take photographs. We climbed and climbed. Trying to stay light and balanced, I took care to place each foot precisely where Robb, in front of me, placed his.

"Robb," I said, "it's too soon for another hike. My muscles are still stiff and sore from the Bright Angel Trail."

Grinning, he said, "No whining. What your muscles need is some activity to stretch them out and warm them up."

High above the river we sat in a carved-out place in the cliff wall for a few moments to listen to Robb talk geology. Too warm, Lana shed her jacket and turtleneck while sitting in the sun. The contrast between her white skin and black bra was startling. There was a moment of silence and she laughed. Mimicking Robb's geology professor voice, she said, "And here's Lana changing clothes!"

I peeled off my splash jacket, stowed it in my pack, and tied my Tevas to dangle from the top strap. In the loose, jumbled rocks, I was grateful for my hiking boots.

Every step was up and up again. My muscles ached, pores sweated, hands swelled and throbbed, heart pounded and lungs burned, but I walked on. At one sharp switchback, I said to Robb, "Good grief, what are you, a mountain goat?"

"Oh, I don't know," he said. "Every step I walked, you walked."

We reached Tapeats Creek and continued our steady climb up the waterway where huge trees shadowed verdant brush. One by one we stepped over a decomposed carcass. Nothing but a pile of bone and dull fur, only the tiny paws identified it as a bobcat. Angie stopped to examine a bat impaled on a cactus spine.

Robb explained, "Predatory loggerhead shrikes catch bats, stick them on the long thorns, and return later to eat them."

"Is it dead?" Gina asked.

"Sure," Robb said, but the bat trembled, its light fleshy wings quivering.

We exhaled a communal groan and moved up the trail, the rhythm of our footsteps sounding out life, death, life, death, life, death.

Coyote Pup

Half hidden in sedges
his carcass melts
back into the earth
leaving beige bones
remnants of fur
and a skull smaller
than my closed fist.

The tiniest teeth peek
from his yawning mouth
and open eye sockets
show nothing of why
he died on the bank
of the shallow river
shy of mid-summer.

Several times we stopped to remove our boots and put on river sandals to cross the boulder-tumbled water of the creek. Some wore tennis shoes and just walked on through, getting wet up to their waists. Robb, Caleb, and Daniel made a human wall across the water and took each of us hand-to-hand to stabilize our footing on slippery rocks in the hard current. We walked through thorny patches of wolfberry, and I stopped to study the large white flowers and deep green leaves of Sacred Datura. We left Tapeats Creek and began the next ascent up to Thunder River.

As agreed, Caleb walked behind me on the trail.

"Get going, gal, or I'm getting out my battery-powered cattle prod," he said.

"The hardest thing for me is now that I've started, I know I can't turn back," I said.

"That's right," he said. "The boats will soon be long gone."

The deafening roar of falling water welcomed us at Thunder River. Hundreds of feet of foam and spray cooled the day, giving us a shady place to sit and eat our lunches. First, though, I stripped off my sweaty T-shirt and dipped in a pebble-lined pool. I splashed and played, delighted that I had hiked so far and felt wonderful. No headache, no upset stomach, no joint pain, no heavy mind-weighing burdens. I squeezed the water out of my blonde braid and stood in a patch of sun, shivering. Far off, masked by the sound of the falls, I heard a few notes of birdsong and listened.

"What is it?" I asked Angie. "An ouzel, or a sparrow?"

"No," she said. "I asked Robb earlier. It's a canyon wren."

"Do you know the Vesper sparrow?" I asked.

"No," she said.

"She has a chestnut wing and white outer tail feather, a

narrow eye ring, and builds her tiny grass-lined nest in open country and lays creamy spotted eggs. Her call is two opening notes followed by several short high trills. She sings in the evening."

"You miss the ranch, don't you?"

"I do, but being here makes me realize how blessed I am at home."

"Do you think John is doing okay without you?"

"I don't know. I hope so. Angie, do you think he'll ever forgive me for going away, for wanting to be here with you?"

"Of course he will. He'll be so glad when you get home, he'll forget all about the leaving part of it. I'm happy you came. I know we haven't had much chance to talk, but I love seeing you here, sharing all of this with me."

"I miss you," I said.

"I know. I miss you too. Don't worry, we'll find time soon to slip off together."

I had eaten my apple on the hike up, but I gobbled down my soggy sweet sandwich along with two fig cookies and long swigs of fresh water taken from the waterfall. I did not know a peanut butter and jelly sandwich could taste so delectable.

I photographed Helen and Gina and Angie clowning around, and Lana snapped a shot of me in my shorts and sports bra sitting in a small pool like a self-satisfied otter. I wanted the memory to take home to John. I soaked my sore feet and dried them with my bandanna and put my sweaty boots back on. Robb gathered his lunch papers and without a word started up the trail again. We fell in line like a bunch of well-trained pack mules.

We met Meg and Shane coming over from the Deer

Creek side, taking the trail in jogging steps to make it along Tapeats Creek to the unmanned boats.

"See you downriver at Deer Creek Falls," Shane said, waving.

"You look great with three and a half miles under your belt," I called to Meg as she increased her pace, keeping up with Shane, her long blonde braid bouncing behind her.

"She's beautiful," Daniel said beside me. "Lean and classy as a racehorse."

I watched him watch her until she disappeared.

"How old do you think she is?" I asked.

"Oh, probably twenty-five, twenty-six," he said. "She amazes me. She helps out with all the work around camp, then rows that boat all day."

"I'd like to ride with her sometime and get to know her," I said.

"You can't," he said. "She's not licensed as a boatman and isn't allowed to have passengers on her boat. This is only her fourth trip down the river."

"Really. She's so at home among the rocks and sand, like an earth spirit. I thought she'd been doing this for years."

Seeing his longing, I said, "You'd like to spend some time with her, wouldn't you?"

"Sure," he said, his smile broadening, "but she already has a boyfriend."

"Oh?"

"Yeah, the night before all of you joined us at Phantom, he hiked all the way down just to spend the night with her, then hiked back out the next morning. Besides," he said, "she's so shy. I can't even get her to talk to me."

Again we climbed.

Lana eased up to me and said, "I feel horrid. I think my

127

toe's infected and my legs are rubbery."

Overhearing her, Caleb put his arm around her and said, "Come on. Lean on me."

I hiked on, glancing back to make sure she had the support she needed.

Caleb teased her. Her laughter made me happy because I knew how much she liked him.

One by one, people dropped back to take photos or grab an extra breath, but I kept climbing, convinced that if I stopped for even a second I'd never start back up again. Shadowing Robb's every step, we encountered twin ravens perched on a rock outcropping. One lifted its wings, croaking out a hoarse caw. I offered a prayer to the wind, whispered "Spirit Bird," and answered the raven in its own tongue. The birds rose from the cliff, sun glinting off black wings.

"Ah, Laurie," Robb said. "Now look what you've done."

"I know," I said without apology. "They'll guide us the rest of the way."

We watched as the pair circled and soared, going higher and higher up the mountain to the top of the rim.

There, looking back and looking forward, we surveyed the entire landscape of castle-shaped walls and deep canyons where every shade of red, brown, gray, and green was represented. Sheer thin clouds drifted past, masking the warmth of the sun for moments before they moved on. We walked a short way across level ground and my calf muscles relaxed. Robb scrambled up the slick side of a huge rounded rock and announced, "This is the highest point on our trek. It's all downhill from here."

Each of us gained the top of the boulder to study the flat expanse of Surprise Valley. Now our challenge would not be climbing, but hiking across the hot dry plain, picking our way through brush and cactus. I took off my cap and put on my bandanna, smeared sunscreen on my arms and face and legs, and kept on walking.

Our group huddled in the coolness of the lee side of Shade Rock and took a brief rest. Somewhere along the trail Robb disappeared. I noticed his absence and kept watch for him. Then, out of nowhere, he was back again at the edge of the gathering, listening to small talk as people shared water and power bars. I peeled and ate my orange, the sticky juice running between my fingers. Robb picked up an apple core someone had thrown down and said, "Hey, folks, pack it in, pack it out."

"Isn't it biodegradable?" I asked, on the verge of discarding my orange peels.

"It's the seeds. We don't want any more invasive species in the Canyon than we've already got."

Angie held out a plastic bag and Robb dropped the apple core in. I contributed the orange peels.

As we trekked on, I surveyed the battered landscape of my legs: dark red scrapes on both knees, a long gash on my left shin, numerous smaller cuts that made it look like I'd been a cat's scratching post, and a colorful array of bruises.

"Oh, God," I said to no one in particular, "I'm going to have a mess of scars."

"Not scars," Robb suggested, "souvenirs."

"What a pleasant thought," I said and scraped the dried blood off the biggest cut.

A mile back I had emptied my water bottle's last sip. Dutton Springs was only a mile ahead, yet the image of water, the taste and feel of water, the sight and smell and sound of water haunted my thoughts as I hiked across the plain. The previous night's rain had dampened the parched

129

earth. I touched a bit of moss in the crack of a rock and was surprised to find it still moist and spongy. Noticing my investigation, Robb said, "It's glad for a drink."

I nodded in reply. The desert was such a beautiful dreamscape of endless textures and unimaginable colors, but without water, without rain, nothing survived.

The Shape of Rain

On a morning ingrained with gray, rain
drops, unable to retain their soft shapes,
clumsily kiss windowpanes, land
as careless as a skein of sandhill cranes
ordained to return to familiar terrain
and claim the greening domain of spring.

Each drop, unaimed, flattens out, wanes,
then slides like the face of a moraine,
finding a plain and separate way to run,
gaining speed on the smooth cool lane
of glass, only to pool constrained on
the main sill, a gathering place for rain.

Puddled on the stained unpainted board
nothing remains of the pear-shaped poise
the rain contained while falling unrestrained,
so like perfect love which entertains and sustains
an intraveining so complete that one is lost
in every other without question, without pain.

We reached a difficult descent in loose rock where the trail turned narrow and steep. Robb called back, "Go slow and watch for slides." Every time he heard a rock roll he stopped and looked around to make certain everyone was still on the trail and making progress. I believed he had 360-degree vision because often he turned just in time to see someone miss a switchback. He would holler, wait patiently. Then pointing, motioned where they should drop down in yet another tough place. Growing weary, I concentrated on putting each foot right where Robb placed his. If footing were safe for him, then it would be safe for me.

Down, down, down we dropped, our knees absorbing the shock of our upper bodies. Robb hummed as he hiked. No particular tune. Just a scattered melody that harmonized with the sounds the earth makes: wind, the crunch of gravel, the slight sound of a rock rolling, of a foot slipping.

"You remind me of an old outfitter, Snook Moore," I said to Robb.

"Who's he?" he asked.

"I wintered with him one year on Tosi Creek in the Upper Green River Valley of Wyoming. Snook hummed too when he worked or when he walked. We fed his horses loose hay out of log cribs all winter. He had to fight off the hungry moose that wandered in the willows along the creek."

"Sounds like an interesting guy," Robb said.

"He was. He didn't have much education, but he taught me to harness, hitch and drive a team, and to drag the meadows after the irrigation water was turned on. He showed me how to shoe horses, repair saddle strings, train a dog to pull a sled, set a marten trap, shoot beaver in the evening when they were out swimming in the ponds, fix fence, and make sourdough pancakes and sourdough chocolate cake."

132

Robb whistled in admiration. "So why'd you leave there?"

"Snook was old enough to be my grandfather. Besides," I teased, "he was married. Did you have a mentor? Someone special who taught you life skills?"

"Michael Jacobs," Robb said. "He was a quiet man, knew the Canyon like the back of his hand. I learned most of what I know about the river from him."

"Is he still living?" I asked.

"No," he said. "Michael died in a fall while climbing in the Tapeats. The Canyon loved and respected him. The Canyon took him for her own.

"Snook still living?" Robb asked.

"No," I said. "He had a sore on his leg that wouldn't heal. It broke open on Halloween night two years ago when he was alone at his cabin and he bled to death. They found him the next day. He was eighty."

"You loved him, didn't you?" Robb asked.

"Yes," I said. "Very much."

Then, we were silent.

Robb stopped, cupping his hand to his ear. Far away, so soft it might have been imagination, we heard the sound of running water.

He smiled and I smiled back.

Evergreen and Roses

Evergreen and roses
for your graveside wreath
the only thing that I could do
to lay you to your peace.

I would have given anything
to hold your hand once more
and let you know you weren't alone
when death came to your door.

But years and miles pushed between
the friendship that we shared
and yet I felt you somehow knew
that I never ceased to care.

It gives me some small comfort
to know you died at home
on the ranch you loved so much
on the land you used to roam.

A tribute to your horseman's life
seemed as easy as a dream
so I harnessed up the team today
and drove them by the stream.

Then I saddled up my sorrel horse
the one you liked so well

the one you said would never buck
but would carry me to hell.

I just moseyed round the pasture
in a bareback trot real slow
to watch the day fade into night
and see the sunset's glow.

It seemed the proper thing to do
to let my mind just drift
and recall the things you gave to me
your cowboy wisdom the rarest gift.

At eighty you were crippled bad
by horse wrecks, work, and years
so I didn't think it right or fair
to shed too many tears.

The cold wind dried my sunburned face
and I promised to carry on
to walk the earth the way you did
before your time was gone.

Lush and shady Dutton Springs appeared like a mirage. People spread out around the rocky cascade, splashing and playing, filling water bottles, eating snacks, lying in the sun. I ambled down to the water and rinsed my hot face.

Watercress grew in luxuriant patches, and Caleb and Lana, sitting together, picked pieces of it to eat. Lana dashed water over her chin-length hair, struggled to untangle the snarls. I took her comb and eased it through her blonde curls, taking care to separate the strands. I ruffled her hair through my fingers, letting the sun and wind do the work of drying.

Stiff and sore from sitting, I waded barefoot in the water to stretch and bend. There wasn't a body part that did not ache and we had several miles to go before reaching the boats. Willpower I had, but my physical strength had ebbed down to zero. I knelt beside the spring and prayed for assistance. In the pebbled pool I caught a glimpse of my wavering reflection.

Portrait of a Woman in Front of Her Mirror

Upswept, her hair holds threads of gray.
Light catches the strands of silver, illuminating her
   age.
She neither smiles nor frowns, just stares serene.

Vague blue veins run under the transparent skin
below the hollow of her throat where a pulse beats,
above breasts weighty and round as unpeeled fruit.

She blinks her eyes and sees who she once was.
Blinks again and sees clearly the woman she is.
Once more, and she's startled at who she'll become.

She reaches up to trace the fine lines around her
   mouth,
the deepening furrows plowed in her broad brow,
seeking in her face some small trace of life's surety.

Refreshed, we hiked on with full water bottles, making our way along the narrow trail, pushing our way through tall stands of bamboo that waved above our heads. At Deer Creek, we crossed by leaping rock to rock. The balanced tightrope dance of crossing rushing water came back to me from my earlier years in Montana. Looking straight ahead, I trotted light and quick, my feet finding the stones. "Good job," Robb said, and I blushed at the compliment. A large dead tree stood on the opposite bank, its dark brown branches reaching up in supplication like a spirit petrified in prayer. We followed Deer Creek downstream where cotton-woods charred by a recent fire still struggled to grow. I reached out my hands to touch the rough blackened bark of the old-timers and looked aloft to see fluttering leaves on the few branches that had survived flames and heat.

Cottonwood Twig

Inside every cottonwood tree
there are at least a million stars
trapped in sap that rises and falls
as surely as the phases of the moon.

If you don't believe me
just take a dry twig from the tree
and pop it apart at a petiole
where slender stem becomes leaf.

What do you see? A five-pointed star
fixed like a fossil beneath the bark,
see it shining, winking and blinking,
set free in the afternoon sunlight.

I love these little wooden stars,
love knowing they are hidden in the heart
of great trees that turn in the constant breeze
blowing along our wide western rivers.

This is what I think: when we burn
cottonwood rounds in winter
we release all its stars into the smoke
that climbs upward into night skies.

Just before Deer Creek disappeared into its deep canyon, we rested again. There, backed up by rocks, swirled a pool powered by a small fall. Tired, shaking, not wanting to risk being wet again, I scrambled high above the water and perched on the lip of a ledge to watch the others splash each other like tipsy teenagers.

"Wish I could bottle that rejuvenating elixir to market back home," I said to Robb, sitting a stone's throw away.

"They'll wear out pretty soon, then we can go on and get you back to a boat," he said.

"You're as indulgent and patient as a parent," I said.

When the last dripping soul emerged from the blue-green water, Robb strode over to the edge of the canyon where the stream vanished. "This way," he said, and walked out of sunlight into deep shadow.

Deer Creek Canyon sported dove gray walls that reached so high only a scrap of sky could be seen. We tiptoed a ledge suspended above the creek and became part of the rock, separated from the sky and the stream by millions of years of weathered erosion. I gripped the wall with both hands to sidle around narrow spots in the trail, watching Robb's every move. I did not look down. I kept my eyes glued to the rock in front of my face and sucked in my breath.

In a sheltered spot where the trail widened, Robb pointed out the fossil tracks of trilobites. White prints of hands and aspen leaves, painted on the reddish rock centuries ago, also decorated the walls.

"The native people blew a mixture of chalk and water through a hollow reed to make the outline of their hands and of the leaves," he said. "The first example of spray paint."

I held my palm up to one of the small handprints and

140

felt the breath of an old one, a familiar feminine spirit, caress me.

"You knew this world the way it was meant to be," I whispered to her. "Your soul did not yearn for another time or place, because you knew no other time, no other place, only your own. I am so tired. I want silence. I want another chance to sit down, but I know if I do, I will not get back up. Can you help me?"

I heard her say, "Walk over to the edge of the ledge and stare down into the darkness."

Curvaceous gray and black walls fell to a thin glimmer of water.

"Now," she said. "Look up."

Far ahead, sunlight illuminated the spot where the canyon opened out into the main river.

"It is not that far now," she said, her voice fading. "You will be all right."

We waited on the rim above the river and looked to Powell's Plateau on the horizon. Our boats, moored on a patch of beach below, floated tiny as a toddler's toys. In the last steep descent, I grabbed rocks and trees whenever I could get a handhold. My strength gone, I struggled to concentrate. No slips. No falls. Robb and Nick and Suzanne walked in front of me, a dozen others behind. It seemed hours before I found flat footing again on the canyon floor.

Looking back, 200 feet above my head, Deer Creek catapulted out of its canyon in bridal-veil ribbons of spray. I sought a spot to sit alone, exchanged my hiking boots for Tevas, and watched while Robb carried Helen piggyback across the cobbled stones to the beach.

Climbing into Hank's boat, I watched people settle themselves, clipping their packs to carabiners, adjusting hats and jackets. I studied the boatmen as they coiled their bowlines. Each had a specific way of untying from a tree or pulling the metal stakes from the sand. Ropes slid through their deft fingers, looping smooth and easy, falling into place like ringed curls in a girl's hair. A slipknot secured the gathered coils and the ropes dropped into buckets in the front of the boats. Then, one by one, the boatmen sprang, leaping onto pontoon sides, bare feet gripping wet rubber, agile as cats. The dance of ropes and hands, the practiced winding and unwinding of bowlines, enchanted me.

Cold and miserable, I donned splash gear for the ride into camp. There were no rapids to run, so Hank entertained us by reading stories from the notebooks he kept in an ammunition can. His voice competed with the river for attention. His was an enduring, solid presence, one tied to the years he'd roamed the backcountry, anchored by the miles he'd charted on western rivers.

We pulled up to a beach just as daylight deserted the Canyon. The Back-eddy was a long meandering strip of sand with hidden nooks and crannies for tent spots. The crew set up the kitchen against the cliffs. Walking a long way to find a good place for our overnight stay, Lana, Helen, and Gina bedded down in a little enclave together near the river. Saying she needed a little alone time, Angie set up her tent apart from them, and I chose a single spot higher up with just a few boulders and a couple of tamarisk trees separating me from Nick and Suzanne. By the time I'd made numerous trips carting gear and tents, exhaustion took over. Gina helped me put up my tent because my arms were so weary I couldn't get the poles to slip into the plastic sockets.

Picking my way through a boulder field, I passed Daniel's half-hidden camp on the way to the river to wash up. When I returned, on the verge of collapse, I sat on a rock with my head in my hands, unable to move.

"Laurie," Angie said, "are you all right?"

Not wanting to talk to anyone, I waved her away.

"Can I bring you some soup?" she asked.

"Maybe I'll come down in a minute or two, Angie, but all I really want to do is crawl into my tent and sleep."

"I understand, but you'll feel better if you eat something," she said.

"Okay, I'll be right there," I sighed.

I dressed warmly and meandered down the path to the kitchen in the near dark. Sipping a cup of soup, and munching on crackers, I drank two cups of hot tea with plenty of sugar.

"Thanks for keeping me going on the trail," I said to Caleb, hugging him from behind.

"No problem," he said, putting an arm around me.

Daniel joined us and we chatted about the day's hike, discussing our worry about the evident infection in Lana's toe.

"She's a pretty woman," Daniel said.

"With a good sense of humor," Caleb added.

"And she's very talented," I said, telling them about her paintings and photographs.

"Where is she?" I asked Caleb.

"Don't know," he said, looking around. "Have you known her long?"

"Just met her five days ago," I replied.

"Oh," he said, "you seem so close."

"I think it's the river," I said, laughing. "Being here puts you in close contact with people really fast."

Lana appeared behind us. "Do you know how odd it is to sit and listen to people talk about you?" she said.

"What were you doing? Eavesdropping?" I asked, hugging her.

143

The four of us filled our supper plates with chili, Dutch-oven cornbread, beans, salad, strawberry shortcake with whipped cream, and plopped down in the sand above the boats to watch the moon rise. Angie, Helen, and Gina squeezed in next to me.

"Talk about companionship," Angie said.

"That's the perfect word," Helen said. "Isn't it amazing that people who were strangers just days ago now seem like family."

Caleb and Lana leaned together, shoulder to shoulder, so I gathered our empty plates for washing and left them alone to talk.

Cornering Stefan, I asked, "How do you guys do this? The quality and variety of food astounds me."

"We've got coolers on board and everything's packed according to how perishable it is; meat's used as it thaws out, fruits and vegetables as they begin to fade."

"What happens to all these luscious leftovers?"

"Sad to say, put in the trash and packed out. Nothing's left behind."

Many people were tired and there wasn't much interest in staying late around the fire. Suzanne and I talked about books and poetry before she headed off to bed. Caleb sat down next to me with his bottle of whiskey.

"Sip?" he asked.

I waved it away. "Not tonight," I said. "I'm having trouble sleeping."

"It might help," he said.

"Nope. I'm so overtired it will just hinder me."

"Have you tried using a mantra to help you sleep?" he asked.

"What do you mean?" I replied.

"A mantra," he said, "repeating something over and over

again, like counting sheep, only better. When you get comfortable in your sleeping bag, try saying this: 'I'm sleeping in paradise. I'm sleeping in paradise. I'm sleeping in paradise.' "

His voice, deep and hypnotizing, made me laugh.

"I'll try it," I said and, using his shoulder for balance, struggled to my feet.

Following Gina's flashlight, she and I wandered back to our camp spots, taking a circuitous route through the trees to find the groover high up on a hill in a rocky nook.

Snuggled in my flannel bag, I practiced deep breathing, but could not sleep. I tried using Caleb's mantra. Over and over again I said, "I'm sleeping in paradise." The wind flapped the tent fly. Rain sprinkled down on and off. As I repeated the phrase, growing sleepier and sleepier, I whispered, "I'm Eve. I'm living in the Garden of Eden. I'm sleeping in paradise." Then, a small voice in the back of my brain said, "Sure now, and where the hell is Adam?" I laughed out loud at my foolishness and slept.

In the middle of the night, I walked down to the river barefooted and waded into the water. The sandy ground was wet with rain, the river full of silver and dark shadows. I found my nylon river pants and my aqua-boots blown downhill by the wind, so I tucked them on a tamarisk branch to dry.

In the darkness, the sound of tent flaps unzipping and zipping told me someone else was awake and wandering around the camp. Lana and Gina ghosted past.

"Where are you going?" I asked.

Startled, Gina giggled, "To wash our hair."

"We can't sleep," Lana said. "The other night we did our laundry by moonlight."

"I'm glad I'm not the only one having trouble sleeping," I said. "See you in the morning."

Portrait of a Woman in Her Bed

Beneath the weight of white sheet and quilted flannel
her heavy calves are squeezed, immobile
with the memory of her morning run up the ridge.

A sharp pain arcs between thick ankle and bulged
    knee
and when she twitches her toes, leg cramps consume
her, the pain, or pleasure, overpowering as orgasm.

She closes her eyes. Her breath catches, caught like
the waxing moon in a web of storm clouds. Exhaling,
she embraces the creamy stream of light falling on her
    breasts.

Everything in her begs to be eased. The open air
    admits
a breeze that caresses her cheek, brushes her hair,
and she slips into unsettled sleep knowing she lies
    alone.

Below Sinayla Rapid

Waking again before first light, I trotted to the groover only to have to wait in line. I heard Hank and Meg working in the kitchen. After packing my things, I begged a hug from Hank, bypassed the delicious-smelling French toast and bacon, and grabbed a banana from the fruit bowl. Sitting in the shelter of the cliff face, I was writing in my notebook when Caleb and Lana joined me.

"Did you get some sleep?" Lana asked.

"Finally," I said. "I'm still fighting some kind of cold or allergy, but Robb was right, the long hike took the pain out of my legs.

"How's your toe?" I asked.

"Better," she said.

"Last call for the groover" rang out.

"Oh, I better get packed," she said to me.

"See you later," she said to Caleb.

"I chanted your mantra last night," I said to Caleb.

"Did it work?" he asked.

"Not exactly," I said. "A strange voice in my head said, 'Yeah, sure, if this is paradise, where the hell is Adam?' "

We laughed together.

There was no thunder to forewarn me, just a bolt. The sudden electric shock of raw desire in Caleb's blue eyes lifted the hair on the nape of my neck. My temperature shot up. The barometer fell and the air turned heavy with promise as lightning looked for a place to strike. Red flags waved and warning bells clanged in my head.

"You're a Scorpio, aren't you?" I blurted out.

"Hey, how'd you know that?" he asked.

I stretched my arms forward, making the sign of a cross like I was warding off the devil, and said, "The worst disasters of my life were due to Scorpio men. You stay away from me!"

"What's so wrong with Scorpio men?" he asked, laughing.

"Oh, nothing," I answered. "They're charming, intense, passionate, daring risk takers who have a dark, secretive side."

"That's me," he said.

"And," I added, "they are prone to destructive affairs which destroy the women who love them."

"That's not fair," he said.

"Tell me it's not true," I challenged.

"So what are you?" he asked.

"Leo, Leo rising," I said.

"Ah, the lioness," he said.

"The lioness, or the shy pussycat," I corrected.

"Which are you?" he asked.

"I'm not exactly sure," I laughed. "I think I've been the shy pussycat for over forty years; maybe I should try being a lioness."

"Do you really believe in signs?" he asked.

"I don't know. Something makes people the way they are. Personalities are formed so early in life. It might as well be the stars, that we are fated to be a certain way."

"It is interesting," he said. "I've been married and divorced twice, and heck if I can figure out why."

"Do you have a girlfriend?" I asked.

"Not right now. Interested?" he asked, his eyes throwing sparks.

"Listen, Caleb," I said, "I like you a lot. You're hand-some and warmhearted. I'll be your friend forever, but I can't afford to have this be more than friendship."

"Done deal," he said and hugged me.

"Oops? Are hugs okay?" he asked.

"Hugs are fine, but let's honor the difference between friendship and romance. I'll feel more comfortable if we set a boundary and don't cross the line."

He hugged me again and said, "I'd better go see if I can help Lana carry her gear."

Seeking out Angie, I invited her to ride with me on Hank's boat.

"I'm envious that you're spending your time talking with everyone else," I said. "Ride with us. I want to hear about your new love, new home, and new life in a new place."

"Okay, let me grab my things," she said.

We settled in the back of the boat, while Suzanne, Nick and Daniel took the front.

"What do you think so far?" I asked Angie. "It's our fifth day."

"I'm doing better," she said. "I feel like I'm opening up more. It's a strange dynamic to find yourself in an un-familiar landscape with people you don't know."

"A landscape you can't leave," I added.

"I know. It's odd, isn't it? I'm still trying to figure out why I'm connecting to some people and not others. There are people here I haven't talked to yet, and I can't even re-member their names. Others I feel like I've known forever."

"You brought some fascinating people into my life, Angie. Robb mesmerizes me with his leadership abilities. Hank's bear hugs are addictive. Kelly's bewitching. Lana's captivating and she's so confident. Gina's sweet and

Helen's childlike glee is contagious."

"I'm glad you like everyone so much. It isn't always easy to know how to get along, is it?" she asked.

"If I've come to understand anything about the Canyon so far, it's this lesson about exploring."

"What's that?" she asked.

"Go slowly. Step softly. Take time to look and listen and feel. Be considerate. Help out. Hold hands. Allow yourself to be immersed in awe. Make reverence a daily ritual."

"It's the perfect prayer," Angie said.

Even with splash gear on, we turned into Popsicles. Floating through a shady part of the Canyon known as "The Icebox," there wasn't even a glimmer of sun. Caleb pulled up beside us in his kayak and asked, "Are you as cold as I am?" We just shivered and nodded.

Hank pointed out a dead sheep on the rocks above the river: a big ram with nearly a full curl to his horns. A yellow-colored scavenger darted away from the rotting hide. Angie stared at the carcass bent back double and asked, "How do you think it died? Do you think it fell?"

"Angie," I said, seeing her distress, "it happens."

"I know," she said, "but it makes me sad."

Obituary for a Wild One

She was down at dawn, flopping
in the road with coyotes tearing
her beige belly hair out in ragged tufts
while a row of ravens envied her eyes.

From her buff-tan color I thought
at first she was your new dun horse,
but she was only an elk struck at night
crossing fences head-on with headlights.

I watched from the window as you ordered
the dog to stay, brushed the ravens away,
and turned her downhill, folding her legs,
but she could not rise or stand or be saved.

For almost an hour I watched you dance
an awkward dance with the half-dead elk,
while her herd, in splendid disarray,
grazed new grass in the horse pasture.

The pistol jerked her up one last time,
then settled her into chilling stillness,
her final breath running red puddles
in the gray gravel and stirred dirt.

Tied behind the green four wheeler
she bounced like a gay marionette,
mimicking her remembered grace,
bounding over dull sage to an open grave.

The next day at dawn I hiked that way
to see coyotes, ravens, and magpies
circling the sweet swollen stench
of her bloated stiff-legged body.

An eagle rose from her hind hoof,
impossibly wide wings pushing the air
into whispers in a silver and pearl sky,
lifting like her spirit into glistering sun.

"Hank," I asked, "how come there aren't any coyotes in the Canyon?"

"Oh, they're here," he said.

"I never hear them," I said. "At home on the ranch, I hear them howl every night."

"They don't travel the main Canyon much," he said. "They stick to the side canyons and flat mesas."

"It seems so unusual not to have coyote song in this remote place," I said.

"I've heard them," Hank said, "just not down here on the river."

We ran a series of small rapids, then two larger ones, Doris and Fishtail, before stopping at Kanab Creek to hike. Rosy, red-brown water showed evidence of a hard rain upstream in the night.

As we walked the creek bottom Robb imparted the history of the area: "This is the place where John Wesley Powell ended his second trip in the Grand Canyon. Kanab, Utah, in the 1860s was a Mormon settlement and was the winter base for Powell. He founded the USGS, the Bureau of Ethnology, which later became the Smithsonian Institution. Powell was interested in the Indian peoples he encountered on his journeys and worked very hard to protect and preserve their cultures."

A dichotomy to describe, narrow, winding Kanab Creek sported bright sun and deep shadow with vegetation sprouting up here and there in sandy spots. Raccoon tracks crisscrossed in the mud. Small purple flowers resembling Colorado's sticky asters bloomed all around. We walked on thin ledges below towering cliffs. Every view, no matter where I turned to look, inspired me. For a few minutes, with no one talking, I heard the Canyon speaking through the water and the wind. My ears registered one faint bird chirp, a small sound in a large amphitheater with perfect acoustics.

Robb took another break to talk geology. I scribbled "unclassified dolomite" in my notebook. While others listened, intent as he pointed out formations and layers of time, I wrote:

"I know nothing about rocks except that I like to touch them, feel their different textured faces, some smooth and cool, some rough and pocked, some slick and hot, some dished and grooved, some round, some sharp. They have personality and inner force. Some are stable and safe, some unbalanced and dangerous. Some have been where they are for millions of years weathering slowly away. Some shifted and rolled and moved, forever altering the landscape.

"With feet and hands, I meet the Canyon rocks on their own terms, getting to know them by feel. I climb over and around and through them. I lean and sit, lie and sleep on them. I slide down rocks like a two-year-old. When no one is looking, I kiss the rocks, pressing my lips to their stony surfaces as if by tasting them, I might know them better.

"I sniff the rocks, and they smell different at dawn than they do at dusk, or in the afternoon when they have absorbed the sun, or in the middle of the night when they are effervescent with starlight. I stand on them to wash, feeling their stability against the river's pushing current. I use small fist-sized ones to hold down my tent, large ones as big as horses as drying racks for my wet clothes. I pat and hug the rocks, and pick up the tiniest ones to fondle with my fingers. I'd always been intrigued with rocks, but here in the Canyon I am immersed in rock, surrounded by rock, inundated with rock, and so I succumb and allow myself to be intimate with rock.

"I hear the rocks breathe and feel a pulsing energy that

154

rushes inside them like blood. I hear them speak. They are hesitant and shy at first, but then a chorus of voices begins talking all at once. The rocks speak a language I do not know, but I seem to understand what they say. Like people from different countries who meet and fall in love, each speaks a tongue the other doesn't know, yet they communicate with hands and hearts and eyes and sighs.

"I admit I've fallen in love with rocks. They know I am inept and inexperienced, yet they love me, too. I have learned what they like most: nakedness, unbound hair, slow movement, soft speech, thoughtful touch, and dreams. Oh, how the rocks love to sleep and dream."

I tried to pay attention while Robb talked, but I wandered among the rocks, my hands seeking the stoic faces of my new lovers. I repeated the beautiful names scientists had given to the rock: Tapeats Sandstone, Bright Angel Shale, Vishnu Schist, Zoroaster Granite, Cardenas Basalt, Shinumo Quartzite. I knew I'd never remember which one was which, but the assonance and consonance, the alliteration and internal rhyme, the metric dance of melody would always be mine. Geology escaped me, like the autumn breeze that rushed over the rocks seducing the summer away, but the poetry remained.

I wrote again: "I may forget their names and maybe even forget their faces, but I'll never forget the way the rocks feel, never forget the indecipherable words they whisper to me when we are alone."

Feeling drained and weary, I wanted to lie in the sun and thaw out, but it was time to go. We hiked out in small clustered groups, and I walked partway with Caleb. At the confluence of Kanab Creek with the river, I saw Lana sitting by herself.

"Where were you?" I asked.

"I hiked out by myself so I could be alone with the Canyon," she said.

"I understand. You're all right?" I asked.

"Uh-huh," she answered, "just cold and tired."

"Me too," I said. "Let's go get something to eat."

I made myself a lettuce, tomato, and avocado sandwich. Taking a handful of chips and a couple of fig bars, I sought the sun and stood in its warm puddle to eat.

Robb called out, "Back to the boats. Got to make some time today."

Despite the sun and cloudless sky, the entire afternoon stayed cold as we floated in the shadow of the walls. Even bailing didn't thaw me out. Hank's skill took us through Upset Rapid with utmost grace. Perched in the front left side of the boat, I gasped when a rock wall rushed toward me. I glanced back. Hank rowed hard to keep us from crashing, his face frozen in concentration. If I had reached out, I could have touched the wet surface of the stone with my left hand, but I was too busy holding on to my black strap and averting my face from the waves.

In calmer water, Hank read for us, selecting pieces from Edward Abbey's *Desert Solitaire* as the chilly miles drifted by. He rowed awhile, then set his oars up and tucked the handles under his knees, and pulled out the book. Once in awhile one of us said, "Hank," and he'd look up to see that we were drifting into an eddy or too close to a beach, and he'd put his book down, take up the oars, and put us back on course.

All the boats pulled over again to go on a stretch-your-legs hike up to the rim and back. Cold and weary, I stayed behind to sit on the rocks in the sun, but a steady icy wind, and the sun's sliding behind the Canyon wall, left me numb and miserable in the shadows. I dug out every piece of clothing in my dry sack and put them on under my splash jacket and pants.

Back on the boat, Angie switched places with Daniel so she could visit with Suzanne and Nick. I asked Hank how many years he'd been on the river.

"This one, or any of them?"

"All together," I said.

"More than I care to say," he said.

I liked the sound of his wry chuckle.

"Are you glad you came?" he asked.

"Yes," I said, "but it's hard adjusting to so many people."

"Seems to me you're doing just fine," he said.

"Well, your hugs have sure helped," I teased.

He smiled and said, "We have to take affection wherever we can get it."

"Would you do the trip again?" he asked.

"Probably not," I answered. "Hope that's not too honest."

"You could do a private trip with fewer people," he said.

"Really? I didn't know you could do that," I said.

"My private permit's coming up next year," he said. "I'm going to take a small group down. We'll take more time camping and exploring, set our own schedule."

"That's something I might do then," I said. "Maybe someday."

When we pulled in to make camp for another night, Lana, Angie, Gina, and Helen picked an area just up from the river in the sand and I marked out a spot above them on a rock shelf. Nick and Suzanne set up their tent just downriver from me so we felt like next-door neighbors. Trying to create some semblance of privacy, we faced our

157

tents away from each other.

Despite being ice cube cold, I walked to the river to splash clean my face and arms. Coming back I saw Angie cradling Gina in her arms.

"What's wrong?" I asked, hearing Gina cry.

"Somehow her sleeping bag got left at the last camp," Angie said. "Lana went to ask Robb if there was a spare one around."

"Gina," I said, "it's not that big of a deal. You can have mine."

"I just want to stay in my tent and be alone," she said.

Helen walked up, bringing her a plate of food.

"Do you want us to stay with you?" Angie said.

"No, just go on. I'll be okay," Gina said.

"All right, we'll check on you after dinner," Helen said.

Soup and hot tea abolished the deep chill that had afflicted me all day. Robb chatted with Caleb as he grilled several dozen pork chops, so I stood nearby listening to the conversation by the glowing fire. Fettuccine Alfredo, made with spinach noodles and Parmesan cheese, along with cabbage slaw and peas, completed the menu. After cleaning my plate, I climbed up the rock shelves to see Gina.

"I'm fine, Laurie," she said. "I just wanted to stay in my little house and read and write. Lana brought me a sleeping bag, so I'm okay. Please don't worry about me."

I searched for the groover in the dusk light and found it hidden at the end of the beach with a slippery rock to scale to reach the spot.

When I walked back by to say good night to Gina, I took her empty plate and silverware back at the kitchen and arrived just in time to have a piece of Dutch-oven chocolate cake that Caleb had concocted using Stefan's instructions.

"You look happy," Daniel said as he came for his own piece of cake.

"I am," I said, licking sticky frosting off my fingers. "It doesn't seem to take much to make us happy here, does it?"

Firelight reflecting off water and sand set an enchanting stage for a poetry reading. Robb began by reciting Wally McRae's humorous "Reincarnation," using Caleb as the second persona in the poem.

I spurred my courage and stood in front of the crowd. Robb leaned forward with his elbows on his knees. Helen sat beside him, massaging Stefan's shoulders. I took a breath and read Hopkins's sonnet, "God's Grandeur," from my scribbled notes:

The world is charged with the grandeur of God.
It will flame out, like shining from shook foil;
It gathers to a greatness, like the ooze of oil
Crushed. Why do men then now not reck his rod?
Generations have trod, have trod, have trod;
And all is seared with trade; bleared, smeared with
    toil;
And wears man's smudge and share's man's smell:
    the soil
Is bare now, nor can foot feel, being shod.

And for all this, nature is never spent;
There lives the dearest freshness deep down things;
And though the last lights off the black West went
Oh, morning, at the brown brink eastward, springs—
Because the Holy Ghost over the bent
World broods with warm breast and with Ah! bright
    wings.

159

The applause and whoops of appreciation encouraged me, so I told the story of the homestead I lived on on the Northfork of the Flathead River when I first came west. Then, I recited my own poem, "Madge":

They say she whacked off her hair
and crammed on a hat,
dressed like a man,
cussed and chewed,
married her hired hands
so she wouldn't have to
pay 'em any wages,
told 'em if they wanted
smokes and booze
to get off their butts
and trap for cash.

When they left, fed up,
she just married another,
outliving them all
until she dropped dead
of a heart attack
in front of the old wood range
while building biscuits.

Forty years later
I still felt her essence
coming down the stairs
into the cold kitchen;
I'd light the lamp quickly
and save the single match
to fire up paper and kindling
carefully set in the stove.

"Move over, Madge," I'd whisper,
"Gonna have pancakes today."

At night her old homestead
house creaked and groaned,
keeping company with the wild
roar of the wide glacial river.
Every spring her crocus
and narcissus bloomed bright
below the south-face windows.

So far from town, no one
close enough to call or visit,
I found myself talking
to her when I was alone:

"Keep the fire goin' Madge,
I'm gonna shovel snow."

"It's all true," Angie told the audience.

"She should know," I said. "Angie lived there too."

Flushed by the fire and exhilarated from reading, I slipped to the sand across from Helen. Robb caught my eye and nodded. Suzanne read several poems, but her soft voice was hard to hear above the roar of the river. Stefan's river riders of the day urged him to finish the remaining chapter of the story he'd been reading to them on the boat. He set a big dry bag near the fire, sat down, leaned against it, opened one of Edward Abbey's books, cleared his throat, and started to read, then stopped.

"Well," he confessed, "I just want you to know I've had a little too much to drink."

He cleared his throat as we laughed and began again.

Caught up in words and images, I wanted to stay by the fire and enjoy the company, but my eyes, drooping, told me to go to bed.

At midnight the moon shone like a spotlight when I walked down to the river. Gina was awake and writing in her tent. Lana, next to her, was awake too. We whispered for a few minutes before I crawled back into my still-warm bed. After repeating Caleb's mantra over and over again, I drifted off into a marvelous dream about a lover coming to me out of the night.

Phantom

Come to me in darkness
and let your lips sing
again our old song
using my whispered name
as sad, soft refrain.

Bury your sunburned face
in my fine flaxen hair
sweet scented with summer
wind-wrestled and unwoven
from the braids that brush
my full but barren breasts.

Lay me against the ground
until I open the earth
with wanton sighs, cries,
the prick of grass and stone
on unsheltered skin
ignites the tinder
between my thighs
fires the night
with lightning need
the quick implosive
updraft of denied desire.

Blanket your charmed body
over mine so I can hear
your breathing build
like waves of wind
rushing across canyon walls.

Bring thick sultry thunder
to shatter the window
of my open soul,
then leave me alone
to count uncountable stars
half a world away
from where you turn and sleep.

Below 164 Mile Rapid
at National Canyon

I dashed down the beach to the kitchen, giddiness riding my shoulders. Caleb leaned against the breakfast table drinking coffee. I threw my arms around him.

"Thank you. Thank you. Thank you. I slept so well," I said, and told him about my dream. "I feel wonderful. It must have been Adam who appeared."

"Damn," he said, hugging me close. "Wish I'd have a dream about Eve."

"I like you," I said. "I like basking in the warmth of your attention and having fun."

"What are you two so jolly about?" Angie said, stretching into one of those "I overslept" yawns.

"I feel good today despite waging war on the allergy thing," I said.

"Here," she said. "Try some of this. Mix it in your tea," and she handed me a packet of powdered electrolytes.

"Are you out of sorts, sweetheart?" Caleb asked Angie, drawing her into a one-armed hug.

"Guess so. I hate being late and having to rush," she said. "According to Stefan there's another long hike planned today."

"You eat, Angie," I said. "I'll make lunches for both of us, then come up and help you pack."

Lana had painted her toenails a shocking shade of pink before the trip.

"It's a fifties kind of pink," she told me, "a color Doris Day would wear."

She had on bright pink lipstick that matched her toes and complemented her fair complexion and blonde hair. She wore a wild-pink long-sleeved shirt that hugged her breasts tight and a bold pink bandanna dangled from the strap of her day pack.

"Oh, don't you look lovely," I said, "just like a hothouse rose. I wish I could look that put-together and pretty."

"You can," she said. "I'm good with color. Where are your clothes? I'll help you."

Rushing, I spilled my meager selection onto a sleep pad and Lana chose beige river pants and a dark green T-shirt with a white bandanna.

"Or," she said, "this ensemble." And she laid out black shorts with a bright blue shirt. "See, the blue stripe on your aqua-socks matches the shirt perfectly. Add that black bandanna for special effect."

I must have looked indecisive. Lana said, "Wear the shorts. It's going to be hot."

I laughed. "Am I being obsessive?"

"No, just having fun. The rustic setting doesn't mean you can't look nice."

"It's silly, but I do want everyone to think I'm attractive."

"Me too," she said. "Hurry up and change. They're loading the boats. I'll help Annie."

Gina joined me at the beach and we climbed onto Hank's boat. He only rowed a short way before the boats pulled into a sheltered cove for the hike up Havasu Creek to Beaver Falls.

"It's a seven-mile stroll," Robb said as we clustered around him in a circle. "We'll be in and out of the stream

166

all day so wear tennis shoes or Tevas."

We climbed a series of steep ledges, shuffled along a narrow path, and crossed the creek before reaching the other side of the canyon where the main trail began. Barefoot, Robb set a fast, steady pace. "This is a stroll?" I said to Angie.

In one spot we lifted our packs above our heads and waded through aquamarine, sparkling-like-a-jewel water that tickled our belly buttons. We crossed and recrossed the creek so many times I lost count. Hoping to keep our balance in the swift water, we grabbed wrists and waded across in a linked chain. In places we clambered around tough spots, squirming through tight places in the rocks, up and over big boulders, along skinny ledges with sheer drop-offs, but mostly we traveled along a gradual incline through wild grapevines that scratched my bare legs.

"Angie," I said when the trail widened enough for us to walk side by side, "today, for the first time, I'm glad I came on this trip. I feel indebted to you, glad you insisted I come."

"Me too. We've been through so much together. You know me. Who I was when I was seventeen, and who I am now. I don't ever have to explain myself to you."

"What's there to explain? You're loving, kind, caring, good at listening, and you never give advice unless someone asks for it."

"You make me sound like a Girl Scout," she said.

"Pretty close," I said. "Are you happy, Angie? Are things working out for you?"

"I'm good," she said. "I do worry about money, but this new relationship feels right to me. We play music together and laugh a lot. We get along. We don't argue. He's good to me, tells me I'm pretty and smart. He tells me he loves me. I need that."

167

"It's such a huge thing, isn't it? Having someone say 'I love you.' "

"It makes all the difference in the world," she said.

Seeing the deep green-blue pool beneath Beaver Falls, I said, "Let's ask Robb if we can skinny-dip."

"Oh, no, let's don't, I'm too shy," Angie said.

"Okay, shorts and bras then," I said.

We stripped partway and waded through the reviving water. In the first pool on the edge of the clearing, I grabbed a handful of mud and scrubbed my scalp clean. Angie and I dog-paddled across a large pool to the falls and Caleb and Lana joined us on the fern-covered ledge. Robb and Meg swam over.

"You can dive underneath the falls into a cavern. It's called 'the green room,' " Robb said.

Then, he disappeared into the roiling cascade. Holding our breath, we watched and waited. Robb shot out of the white foam like a spawning salmon and was swept downstream. He swam hard for the opposite shore, climbed out on the cliff, and sat dripping in the sun.

Caleb and Meg braved the waterfall dive.

"Not me," Angie said.

"Me either," I added. "Lana?"

We watched Caleb and Meg pop out of the water. "Guess not," she said.

We squatted on the moss-covered shelf and slipped back into the water, swimming with long strokes for the cliffs. They both grabbed the wall, but I was being swept towards the lower falls when Angie latched on to my hand.

"Thanks," I said as we scrambled out of the water, chilled and shaking. "That was a rush. What if you hadn't rescued me?"

We looked at the roaring mass of water and rock below.

"Don't even think about it," Angie said.

We stayed only long enough to retrieve our breath, then swam back to where our packed lunches waited.

Angie huddled against the wall, shivering. Worried about her blue lips, I rubbed her arms and legs to increase circulation. The sun beat down. Cozy and content, I wanted time to stand still as I shook out my hair, fluffing it in the breeze, then ate my squashed sandwich and crumbled cookies. Angie, Lana, and Caleb sat in a circle on a scant patch of grass. Robb stretched out in a slant of sun with his hat over his face and I wondered if he slept.

"Lana?" I asked, motioning to her.

She walked over and I whispered, "Will you take a photo of me by the gold and red rock wall behind that clump of trees? I want something seductive to take home to John."

"Sure," she said, getting her camera.

"Caleb," I said, as we walked past, "don't turn around."

He grinned at me and said, "Okay."

In the relative seclusion of the sheltering trees, I pulled off my sports bra, rumpled my wet hair into curls, and smiled a siren's smile.

"Raise your arms above your head," Lana directed. "It will make your breasts look firm and round."

"I'm nervous," I giggled.

Lana snapped several shots. "You look great. This honey-colored light is perfect. Hold still. Couple more.

"So," she said as I put my bra back on, "you're a secret exhibitionist."

"Is that what it's called when you want to walk around half-naked?" I asked, laughing.

"That or sexy, sassy, sensual. You pick."

"All I know is that it feels delicious. Like being free in a new way."

169

"What were you two up to?" Caleb asked as we rejoined the group.

"Oh, nothing," we laughed, hugging each other.

I slipped on my dry T-shirt, struggled out of my soggy bra, then clipped it to the back of my pack to let it dry in the wind.

"Time to head back," Robb said, indicating that the sun had dropped behind the rock walls.

We gathered our things and Meg took the lead for our return. As I walked past Robb on the ascent up the side of the cliff, he reached out and ruffled my wet hair. "Water sprite," he said, grinning, and it made me smile.

Caleb and Lana hiked together, their heads close, talking. Angie seemed pensive and tired, so I teamed up with her, and we walked side by side in silence.

The notion of nakedness played in my mind. It was becoming an accepted state of being for me in the Canyon. Going to the river to relieve myself or to bathe, I had to share the limited beach space with others. Often there was only a jumble of boulders or a thin patch of trees between nakedness and the rest of the camp. No one minded or cared. I was learning the simple art of turning my head or walking on by to allow someone else a measure of privacy.

I thought of the evening after the boats were unloaded, beer passed out, and supper preparations underway, when I saw Robb strip down on his boat and dive into the river. When he came up for air, his bottle of camp suds close to hand on the edge of his boat, he lathered and rinsed, dunking himself again and again, as the sun began its descent. He toweled himself dry and dressed in clean clothes before joining the rest of us for the evening meal.

One morning, as his boat drifted away from camp into a

170

quiet stretch of the river, he set the oars securely, grabbed his well-used cup, dipped it full of river water, and stood there brushing his teeth as the Canyon walls slipped by. It was a reverent moment. All of us with him on the boat stayed silent as if observing a minute of prayer while he finished his ablutions. He snapped the water from his toothbrush, stowed it away, dipped another cup of water from the river, and drank deeply. He swiped the back of his hand across his bearded face and sighed, "Ah, now I can start the day."

One of the Canyon's great gifts to me was the sheer, simple beauty of being clean and naked.

The group stopped just above another creek crossing for a breather. My hands and fingers were swollen and beginning to hurt. I raised my arms above my head, stretching to ease the ache. I tried twirling my wedding band, but it pinched tight, constricting the blood flow in my left hand.

"What makes our fingers swell here?" Nick asked me.

"I don't know," I said. "Maybe it has something to do with salt intake and hydration or altitude and humidity."

When Robb walked up, I asked him. His face serious, he pondered a moment, then said, "It's the sign of an immoral past."

Several silent seconds passed before everyone burst into laughter. Solemn, I raised my right hand and said, "I hereby confess to an immoral past."

"We knew that," Lana shouted.

"One good thing about my immoral past is that I have nowhere to go but forward toward a more moral future," I countered. "If I'd been perfect then I'd have nothing to strive for."

We hiked on, Suzanne falling in beside me. I raised my

arms above my head as I walked, then lowered and shook them hard. Suzanne followed suit.

"What are you doing?" Helen asked.

"Ridding ourselves of our immoral pasts," we answered.

Reaching the boats, we loaded up in radiant sunshine to float the nine miles to camp at National Canyon. Soon, though, the sun disappeared behind tall walls. Cold, wet, and tired, my fine day had turned to blank misery. Hank noticed. He pulled a bottle of apricot brandy out of a box and passed it to me.

"Mum's the word," he said.

The first, pursed-mouth sip burned down my throat, thawing out my tight chest. The second slid down smooth and warmed me to my toes.

"Tell me about you," I said to Hank. "Where do you live? Are you married? Do you have kids? Where did you grow up?"

He chuckled and while relaying answers he recited snippets of Shakespeare, the Bible, and Dylan Thomas. I played with him, reciting sonnets and the prologue to *Romeo and Juliet*.

"Do you often find lovers of classical literature on the river?" I asked.

"Sometimes," he said. "And then you've found a true companion."

"Which contemporary writers do you like?" I asked.

"Oh, Stegner and Stafford. Ed Abbey, of course. How about you?"

"I'm in love with Isabel Allende and James Tipton right now."

"Don't know them," he said.

"Such wonderful words. The exploration of the sensual, finding delight in the everyday experience," I said.

172

"Sounds like you," Hank said.

"Not at the moment. Hank, I'm so cold I think I'm going to die."

"Hang on, gal," he said, handing me the brandy again, "we're almost home."

Poets

Seduced by the sound of words,
poets spar, grappling like gods
over the love of language.

They wrestle the worst of themselves
against the best of others
hoping to gain a hold on understanding.

Unable to live without reflection,
they look in mirrors searching
for a twin face, a like heart.

First on the beach, I picked a spot for us at the edge of camp not far from the river. I carried in sleep kits and pads, and helped set up tents. Meg came with the groover.

"Do you mind?" she asked.

"Not in the least. If it's close, I won't get lost in the dark trying to find it."

She smiled and took a small trail on the side of my tent to place the groover back in the trees along the side of a wash beneath the Canyon walls.

I hung my wet clothes in nearby trees and rolled out my sleeping bag before dark. As the sun disappeared, I wandered through thigh-high boulders to wash my face at the river.

Served by torchlight, our supper included enchilada casserole, Spanish rice, corn, refried beans, and guacamole. Caleb and I sat in the sand together to eat.

"What's up?" I asked. "You seem preoccupied."

"It's Lana," he said. "I might be falling in love."

"Good for you," I said, patting his arm.

"I don't know. She's absolutely beautiful. Fun and flirty. Yet, she's confusing as hell. When I try to be more affectionate, she withdraws. I don't get it, do you?" he asked.

"I haven't known her much longer than you have," I said, not wanting to divulge confidences Lana had shared with me about her childhood and the dissolved marriage.

"I do know she likes you a lot," I added, poking him in the ribs, "we all do."

"Women always like me," he said, "then they dump on me."

"That wouldn't have anything to do with your behavior patterns, would it?" I teased.

"Don't be so hard on me," he groaned. "My heart is at risk here."

"What? You're not willing to invest again if you think there might be a wreck?" I asked.

"Quit joking. I'm at a loss. I'd just like to be successful for once. Come out the winner," Caleb said, wrestling me playfully.

Walking by, Robb heard us. He stopped, shook his head in disbelief, and mumbled a string of curmudgeonly cuss words about men and women and walked off.

"Well," I said, "I guess he told us exactly what he thought about the subject."

After washing dishes, I begged a big bear hug from Hank and asked him to stay up and read to us.

"No, Chicky," he said, "I feel shy in that big of a group. Besides, if I don't go to bed early, I won't wake up to fix you breakfast at dawn."

"How do you sleep with all the noise in camp?" I asked.

"I put on my Walkman," he said, "and listen to music."

"Really, who's your favorite singer?"

"Patty Loveless," he answered.

"Oh, she's my husband's favorite too," I said.

"That figures," he said.

"You'd like him, Hank. Of all the people in camp he'd like you the best because you two could talk about the land, and cattle, and ranching," I said.

"And rivers," he added.

"Yes, and rivers," I said and gave him another hug.

At the campfire, Suzanne told tales about bagpipes and Scotland. She played her chanter, and taught us to sing a Scots song. Robb joined the circle and stood by me, his voice rich, warm, and in tune as he sang. His calm energy settled me, gave me the pleasant sensation of feeling grounded and secure.

176

I wore a long, loose, over-the-hips fuzzy purple fleece jacket that had pink ribbons at the zippers and my purple-and-black patterned tights.

"You look like a California grape," Robb said.

"Thanks," I said, laughing. "At least you didn't say I looked like a California raisin, all dried-up and shriveled."

"I wouldn't dream of it," he said.

"Read for us, Robb?" I asked.

"I will if you will," he said.

"Okay," I said, and he jogged to his boat to get his books.

By firelight we read from his David Lee books, swapping poems and making comments. Our audience loved it and as the whiskey and tequila made the usual rounds, things grew quiet and mellow and easy.

"And now," Robb said, the liquor smoothing out his voice, "as a coda to that performance, I'm going to recite for you 'Whang Leather.' This is just a little poem about how God made man with just a little extra piece of whang leather hanging from his belly, and how he made woman with just a little piece of whang leather missing between her thighs."

He stepped up to the fire, squared his shoulders and re-cited the ribald poem. Everyone cheered. "And, that," he said, "in closing, is the story of why men and women need each other to be complete."

People drifted away to their sleeping spots. The moon rose, full, bright, and beguiling.

"We're going to walk up National Canyon," Robb said by way of invitation.

"Let me go get my boots on," I said. "Be right back."

Five of us, Helen, Daniel, Nick, Suzanne, and me, fol-lowed Robb into the secluded place: silence, white rock,

177

wet gravel crunching underfoot, running water shining darker than the stones we stepped on, pools reflecting back ethereal light, walls that looked like carved monuments with faces.

We scrambled over and around boulders and along ledges. In the semidarkness, the sensations of danger and excitement held hands. Wound up, Helen chattered like a first-grader. Robb helped us in tough places and Nick kept Suzanne on track. Slow step by slow step we made our way into the heart of the canyon.

Whispering, Robb said, "A major flood swept through the canyon a few years before, leaving boulders the size of small houses that choked off the stream and backed up the water into stagnant lakes. Last year another flood pushed the rocks aside, opening the canyon again into this clear stream and the pools."

We reached a white rock ledge. Perfectly smooth underfoot, it felt as cool as satin to my hands when we lay down side by side, letting a smaller ledge serve as a pillow. We looked up at the thin slice of night sky caught between the lips of the canyon walls. Star shine and moonlight glimmered off the rocks up high. Drawing on their knowledge of astronomy, Daniel and Robb pointed out the constellations. We laid there a long time watching the light shift shadows, listening to the sound of running water, and to our own breathing.

National Canyon

The full moon
leaves her naked
strips away velvet
and silk shadows
until there is only
bare rock and sheer water
shivering under my steps.

I try not to stare,
but my eyes are everywhere
glued to the glistening silver
of limestone skin
the changing expressions
on her white face.

Deep within, unseen,
I hear the source of a flowing stream,
the light long wind of a sigh,
a soft muted moan
that says she's waiting.

"I'm going for a swim," Robb said. "Anyone else want to go?" he asked.

At first no one responded, but I struggled to my feet whispering, "I will."

I followed Robb into the darkness, then I heard the others coming behind us. At the very end of the canyon a pool of black water glistened, lapping against a gravel bar. We undressed and slipped into the cool water, Robb first, then Helen, and me, Daniel, and Nick. Suzanne waited onshore.

The bottom of the pool disappeared from underneath my feet, forcing me to swim. The air felt eerie and I pulled long strokes with my head out of the water so I could keep Helen's back in sight. One by one, we clambered over a boulder blocking a narrow part of the canyon, then swam again, dog-paddling between slick rock walls, the water bottomless, with just a sliver of bright sky to guide our way. We gasped and laughed until finally our feet found rock and our hands reached out to grip the sides of the confined space.

Robb climbed, water sheeting off his lean body. He stuck his butt on one sidewall and planted his feet on the other and squirmed along high above a murmuring waterfall. My pulse racing, I watched Helen copycat follow him. I did not want to go any farther, but Daniel boosted me from behind and I grabbed for the walls. My wet skin clung to stone. Helen and Robb disappeared around a corner. I swallowed and took a long, slow breath. Inch by inch, I slid forward, looking back to make certain Daniel and Nick were following.

We wedged ourselves in the rocks high above the falling stream and stayed there, lined up like moonlit spirits. Our voices, when we spoke, were soft and slow, harboring slight echoes. Helen trembled from the cold, so Robb and I moved in closer to share our body heat. Daniel and Nick sidled over and we stayed tucked together. Time passed. We did nothing but breathe and sigh and stare upward at the sky.

I crossed my arms, cradling my breasts, and tucked my hands in my armpits. My rump numbed and feeling in my feet evaporated. The cold burned, intense inside every pore of my skin that opened to the moment. I ached to say, "So this is bliss," but kept my words safe within.

Robb signaled our descent, then magician-like he clawed his way higher up the face of the cliff and arched above us like a suspension bridge so he could watch and make certain we all made it safely down.

I did not want to leave. Helen scooted over me and followed Daniel and Nick. I heard a body splash into the pool. For a long moment I was alone with rock and water and the woman I had lost such a long time ago.

Worship the Goddess

I will worship the goddess within if I must,
envying her essence, living only to trust
the voice yet unheard, the soul still unseen,
coveting power caught in the brave scream
of self that blows my body back to breath,
that first enchantment suckled at the breast
of being what I am, an outward wave
that waits to rush into her sacred cave.

I will love the woman harnessed to the task
of living wretchedly behind the painted mask
of female failing, my imperfect skin.
I'll love wholly, forgetful of my sins,
tryst with tears and honor the blood I bleed,
love myself, and embrace my darkest needs.

Shaking, I slipped down the dark walls and pushed off into the pool. I heard Robb swimming behind me, so I waited on the gravel bar, dripping in the moonlight, to help him out. He grabbed my hand, held it while we walked a few steps, and whispered, "Thanks."

Quivering from the cold, I dried off with my bandanna, dressed, and shoved damp feet into socks and boots.

As we started back down the trail, I swished my hair to help it dry. Robb walked up behind me and ruffled the long strands.

"Wet again," he said. "That's twice in one day."

I laughed and pushed him playfully away.

The group stayed close walking together out of the canyon, Helen whispering to Robb, Nick telling Suzanne about the swim, and Daniel and I, both quiet, bringing up the rear.

Robb stopped again at the limestone ledge. He turned in a circle, looking at the canyon from every angle. Then, he lay down. Helen settled on his left side and I on his right. Daniel stretched out beside Helen, and Nick and Suzanne lay near me. I shivered inside my skin, but the rock felt warm and I could feel the earth breathing beneath me.

"Oh guys," Helen said, in her light lovely voice, "let's all hold hands."

Daniel held Helen's and she held Robb's and Robb held mine and Nick and Suzanne, an arm's length from me, held each other's. In the near quiet, the sound of the water and wind hummed a lullaby.

For the longest time, we rested, not moving. I wanted to turn and look at Robb, but I was afraid he might be looking at me. So I closed my eyes and breathed deep until my pulse slowed and my mind cleared. When I finally rolled my neck to the side to look, Robb's eyes were shut, beads of water still clinging to his beard, and his left hand was spread open on his chest, his gold wedding band glinting in the moonlight. I began to tremble, and he turned to face me.

I watched him open his eyes and did not look away. His hand relaxed in mine and I brushed my thumb over his rough knuckles. For a second his grip tightened, then he released my hand.

"Let's go," he said, and reached down to help both Helen and me stand.

The moon peered over the rim, and we walked the rest of the way in silver light bright as day. We met Meg going up the canyon on her own. She waved, but did not stop. In the tall brush close to camp, I waited behind Helen to give Robb a hug. He smelled of earth and whiskey and wood smoke when I wrapped my arms around him.

"Thank you," I said, my mouth close to his ear. "Thank you for being the man you are."

"Sorry about that," he said, leaning back to look at me.

"What do you mean?" I whispered. "There's no need to apologize."

Helen grabbed my hand and led me away. As we walked toward our tents, I looked back for Robb. He was working his way through the rocks, returning to the canyon. If Helen hadn't been holding my hand, I would have followed him.

Buoyant as a girl who had skipped school, Helen chattered. "Oh, that was so much fun. Wasn't it incredible? Let's keep it as our secret, okay? Don't tell the others about our adventure. I don't want to have to explain anything to anyone."

In my silk long johns and fleece jacket, I thawed out, but my chest squeezed tight and I coughed and could not sleep. I pulled my flannel bag out into the moonlight and lay there

184

thinking about all the hands I'd held in the Canyon, how we helped one another get up from our soft seats in the sand or assisted each other in and out of the boats. While hiking, outstretched hands reached to pull me up a difficult place or guide me down a tough spot and a chain of hands guided me across hard-current creeks. Walking with the other women to bathe, it was the most natural thing in the world to hold hands and share the ritual of washing like lovers. I never reached out my hand that someone, man or woman, didn't take it, hold it, give it a quick squeeze, or pull me into an embrace. In this unknown environment, holding someone's hand meant a moment of sheltered harbor where I felt safe.

I could still see our hands reaching for one another going up National Canyon. Helen holding my hand as we walked those first steps in the moonlight. Robb reaching back from a boulder to grab Helen's hand and help her up and over. Daniel when he squeezed my hand to reassure me before starting the descent of the waterfall. My hand reached out, waiting for Robb on the edge of the pool to help him make the transition from water to rock. Nick never let go of Suzanne's hand. Every second, with every step, he held on to her.

I could still feel the rush of energy flowing through our clasped hands as we lay on the limestone ledge looking at the stars. Cool and hard in mine, Robb's hand was an extension of the rock beneath us, a landscape in itself. It felt as old as the earth, the calluses on his palm tough and weathered as the Canyon walls, the short smooth nails polished as driftwood by sand and water, the knuckles rough and dark as lava rock. Yet, in between each finger and in the fleshy fold of skin connecting his thumb to his forefinger, the skin was soft, sensitive tissue that breathed, inhaling and exhaling the very air.

I folded my hands across my chest as the moon disappeared behind the rim. Its light faded and the stars reappeared. Beginning to fall asleep, I felt someone's hand there holding mine.

"Dad?" I whispered. "Adam?"

Last Dance

In darkness common to the change of night to day,
I walk on frost-refracted stars spilled from the sage
and hear unseen the whistled south migrating wings
of ducks near where the slow bent freezing river sings
that winter waits impatiently before she seals
the land with snow and begs a ragged coyote steal
short summer's soft and simple tune, then turn with
   trick
long howls into that chilling melody. Too quick,
too fast the change of living life to death, the pure
bother of just breathing scrapped and set to rest, your
fine face shrunk from the flesh you left with no regret
and in your leaving marked the steps I can't forget.
So, where rising sun and setting moon light meet,
I dance an awkward dance with you on silvered feet.

Below Whitmore Wash

"Friday, the thirteenth of October," I wrote in my notebook. "Dragged down and tired. I shouldn't have gone swimming and allowed myself to get so cold."

I couldn't be upset for long because over breakfast Helen and I giggled about our midnight escapade. Daniel slipped up and gave us both hugs. Nick stopped to pat us on the back. Suzanne whispered, "Such fun. I'm so glad I was along to feel the magic."

Hank served Mexican food for breakfast, scrambled eggs with chiles, salsa, refried beans, and warm tortillas. After washing my dishes, I walked back to my secluded site to finish packing and found Robb sitting on a rock waiting for the groover.

"Are you in line?" I asked.

"Waiting patiently," he replied.

I sat on the ground next to him and he put his hand on my shoulder.

Silent, we sat and watched as everyone packed up the kitchen and prepared to leave. When Robb returned from the trees, he handed me the signal cushion so I could retrace his route.

"Carry these down for you?" he asked, pointing at my tent bag and sleep pad.

"Sure. Thank you," I said.

I waited for him to say something else, but he waved and went on.

Before loading the boats, the entire group hiked up National Canyon. Daylight painted the scene in different light. The setting seemed too real compared to the night before. Robb remained pensive. Helen and I held hands again, whispering night secrets. Lana joined us. Then Caleb trotted to catch up too.

When we reached the far end of the canyon, Robb sat on a rock and watched while Caleb climbed above the falls, until he could go no farther and had to turn back. Nick decided to swim the same route we'd taken at midnight and this time Suzanne undressed to follow his lead. Robb grinned and waited for them to return. Slow and uncomplicated, the morning eased by.

Returning to camp, all we had to do was don our life jackets and gather day bags. Gina and I had never ridden with Shane so we climbed into the back of his boat while Nick and Suzanne rode in the front. An uneasy excitement foreshadowed the afternoon because Lava Falls was on the agenda.

Gina and I chatted with Shane, peppering him with questions. He was thirty-two now, on the river for eight seasons, engaged a few years back, but his wife-to-be wanted him to give up the Canyon and stay at home. He couldn't quit the river and be happy, so he called off the wedding. During the winter months he installed drywall, a trade he learned from his uncle. He also credited his uncle with opening the world of rivers and water to him by teaching him to kayak at a young age.

"I messed up my shoulder in a kayak accident and had to have surgery, so I gave up kayaking for boats and the Colorado River," he said.

"Have you ever had a trip from hell?" I asked.

"Yep," he said, "a father and three children who complained about everything: the weather, the mosquitoes, the food. I hate this, they'd say, coming through the supper line. They bitched and moaned, left their clothes and gear on board my boat. They never pitched in or helped out."

"What did you do?" Gina asked.

"I got fed up," Shane said. "I threw a screaming fit and said, 'I hate my job: I hate cooking and I hate doing dishes and I hate setting up camp and I hate rowing and I hate all of you.' Then, I jumped in my boat and rowed away, leaving them stranded with the other guides."

"Did you get fired?" I asked.

"No, but I certainly made an impression on everyone."

"What about a trip from heaven?" Gina asked. "Ever had one of those?"

"Oh, yeah," he said, "this past spring when I met my sweetheart, Stacy."

"Is it serious?" I asked, not caring that I was being nosy.

"Yep. She moved out west from Boston and she's working as a wrangler on a dude string until I finish this season," he said.

"I bet you miss her," Gina said.

"Oh, do I ever," he said.

On the Back Burner

Love, slow simmering
on the lowest possible heat,
makes the most hearty,
savory soup for the soul.

Safe cooking, no need
for watching or stirring,
that constant eye of concern,
so gentle, lid on,
no risk of boiling over
steaming dry
scorching around the edges
or burning itself black
in flurried rush and hurry.

Oh, the time it takes!
The waiting, the wanting,
the gnawing hunger that
moistens our mouths
keeps us breathing deep
the spicy smells of desire.

Hearts in hand
we taste and taste again,
certain and sure
that soon enough
when love's finally ready
eager and anxious
faint and famished
we'll dine.

"Shane?" Gina asked, "How did you get your name?"

"From the character in the book and the movie. I never forgave my mother for that. As a kid everyone teased me, calling after me, 'Shane, don't go. Shane, come back, come back!' "

"I think it's a neat name," I said. "I'll bet Stacy likes it.

"Are you as cold as I am?" I asked Gina.

"Yes. It feels worse than yesterday," she said.

"Don't worry," Shane said. "You'll warm up when we hit Lava Falls."

The boats stopped above the falls so the boatmen and kayakers could scout the rapid. Gina and I stole upriver for a bathroom break. Then, we walked to the top of the black cliffs to look down at the rapids with all the others. Energy, high-geared and giddy, pulsed around us. Everyone was nervous, putting me on edge. Caleb's eyes were apprehensive. I hugged him, pecked him on the cheek. "Take care," I said.

I hugged Stefan and Meg and Hank. Everyone sounded upbeat, but a tinge of worry hovered above the smiles and slaps on the back.

The kayakers paddled toward the falls. One by one, mere flicks of color against the silver-green water, they vanished.

The first boat in line, Shane pushed off from shore. No one spoke as we drifted into the main current. I ran my fingers over the delicate face of the river.

"Grant us safe passage," I prayed. Then held my breath.

Shane turned the boat slightly sideways and we scooped down into the roar of froth and foam. Nick and Sue, inundated with water, screamed in unison. Trying to straighten the boat, Shane lost an oar for a split second, regained control, and we were sucked back into the maelstrom.

Gripping the black strap, spreading my feet wider to keep my balance, my sense of direction disappeared. Water was everywhere, but no air. The noise, like a night train rumbling over a trestle, disappeared. Pervasive silence echoed in my ears. I didn't know if I was on the boat or in the river. A deep blackness punctuated with flashing light was the only thing I could see.

Then, the roar of the river returned. I heard Shane exhale, like a whale sounding. Nick and Suzanne yelled. I felt the boat sigh and settle, slow into a gentle rocking. I didn't realize I had my eyes shut until I opened them and saw Gina, grinning, reaching out her free hand to me. I grabbed it.

"We made it," she said.

"Thanks to Shane," I said, "and to the river spirit that listens to prayer."

"Here's to Shane," we all shouted.

"Here's to all of you," he said, standing up to look back at Lava Falls. "Thanks for hanging on."

With the rapid leveled out, Shane turned the boat so we could watch Meg coming through alone. The kayakers lined up in quiet-water formation, waiting to help her if she had trouble. Seeing that tiny figure, just a glimpse of blonde hair and red shirt on a blue boat, flashing through the waves, made my heart stop. I couldn't believe we'd come through that explosion of water.

Safe below the churning swells, Meg pulled over to bail out her boat. The kayakers circled her and cheered, raising their paddles in salute. One by one the rest of the boats bucked through the granddaddy rapid and lined up, waiting for Robb, last in line, to take the plunge.

Invoking every divine being I knew, I whispered, "Keep him safe."

Gina squeezed my hand harder. Angie, Lana and Helen were on Robb's boat.

The speck of blue dipped down into the lip of the falls, and then ceased to be. It was as if the boat had never been there at all. I whipped off my sunglasses and strained to see into the sparkling waves.

"There," Gina shouted. "There they are."

The boat bobbed into sight, everyone still on board. Even from far away I saw Robb standing in the well, heard his shout of glee. All the boats and kayaks waited while Robb rowed past. The boatmen called his name in rhythmic unison, their salute to the trip leader who had seen them and their guests safely through the toughest part of the journey.

Around the next bend, Robb tied his boat to a small cliff where a cascade poured into the river. He climbed and stood in the waterfall to fill five-gallon water cans. Shane hooked our boat to Robb's and I began to bail out the water taken on going through Lava Falls.

Spirits were high and laughter spilled from every group. Lana, bailing Robb's boat, threw a scoop of water at me. Then, I threw one at her. She retaliated. I scooped up another bucketful and she pointed up at Robb. I dashed the splash at him, laughing, but he scowled back, making me feel like a scolded child. "Sorry," I mouthed and quit messing around.

The boats pulled back into the river's main current and drifted a few miles before we pulled over to have lunch on a beach. Gina and I stripped off splash gear and hung it in trees to dry before we strolled down to make our sandwiches. The sun appeared from behind the clouds, a brief incandescent gift, before it disappeared behind the canyon walls. I jumped up and down, but couldn't warm up or thaw out, couldn't be calm after the exhilaration of the Lava Falls run. I paced up and down the sand hills and ran along the beach, holding my throbbing hands at waist level.

Exposed to wind and water, sun and stars, fire and sand, sticks, stones, and dishwater, my hands were disintegrating in the Canyon. So often wet, then dry, they cracked, split, and bled, so painful I couldn't hold my hairbrush or tighten the straps on my dry bags. No matter how much lotion and sunscreen I slathered on them, they hurt.

Hank waved me over to the warm patch of sand where he sat, finishing his lunch.

"Sit down," he said. "Stay put."

He walked over to his boat and returned with an almost-empty bottle of Super Glue. His hand steady over mine, he squeezed one crystal drop after another into the raw cracks, repairing the rents in my flesh.

"Don't move," he said, "or you'll stick your fingers together." A drop fell close to my wedding ring.

"Uh-oh," I joked, "don't make that a permanent attachment."

In seconds, the liquid hardened. In minutes the pain was gone, and I could flex my fingers again.

"Hank, I hate being a wimp, but I'm falling apart. It's not just my hands," I said. "I'm tired, my throat hurts, I have a headache, my back's stiff, I'm bruised all over, and my legs look they've been run through a meat grinder."

"But you still look beautiful, even when you whine."

I hugged Hank and kissed him on his whiskered cheek.

"You're just the best medicine, Hank. Thank you," I said, and shuffled off to find Gina.

Robb called, "Load up," and we headed down the river. After a few short and easy rapids, the water stretched out long and flat. Shane rowed mile after mile. He dug around in one of his boxes and came up with a bottle of Advil. He dumped several pills in his hand and swallowed them without water.

"What hurts?" I asked.

"My shoulder," he said.

"The one you bunged up and had surgery on?" I asked.

"Yeah," he said.

"I can work on it for you later on," I said.

"You should let her do it," Gina said. "Laurie has good hands."

Shane's boat was the first to tie up below Whitmore Wash. Gina and I unloaded our gear, thanking Shane for such an amazing day. As he walked up the beach with a folding table, we called after him, taunting, "Shane, don't go. Shane, come back, come back!" He raised his empty arm and we laughed.

"Was he letting us know he heard us or giving us the finger?" Gina asked.

"Not sure," I said, laughing. "But I know he knew we were kidding."

We picked out a nice spot above the kitchen to camp. When the other women arrived, Gina, Angie, Lana, and Helen created an enclave to themselves, while I sought out a site a bit separate and apart, a place just big enough for one tent so I wouldn't have company too close.

I needed rocks around me, and a few trees, so I felt sheltered, so I'd have a place to hang things to dry. I wanted a smooth flat stretch of sand where I could position my bed with my head uphill. I didn't have to choose a view because every direction I looked was too exquisite to describe. I wanted to be close enough to the river so I could walk there easily to wash, but far enough away so that I didn't infringe on anyone else's privacy.

The location I selected was protected on two sides by rocks and trees, but I intruded into a lizard's living room.

"Excuse me," I said. "I didn't know this place was already taken."

He skittered to a higher rock and watched me unpack, his tongue flicking out.

"Do you mind if I stay?" I asked.

He moved to another rock, and investigated an aqua-boot. Then, leapt to the tree where I hung my splash jacket, pants, hat, bandanna, and glasses. I quit moving about, knelt down, closed my eyes and just breathed for several minutes. When I opened my eyes again he was still there, his prehensile toes gripping a black branch. I felt like an interloper and wondered if I should move my camp some other place. The lizard looked at me. I sighed and asked out loud, "Do you want to share your space?" He dipped his head and zipped away, so I took that as permission to stay.

Lost Maples

I lie like a lizard on a limestone ledge above a water
   hole
and watch a woman walk along the stream in wading
   slippers
and a yellow suit, her skin as white as the light
reflecting off the face of the pool where a school
of small striped bass circle slick rocks.

The sun swallows sweat as it seeps to the surface
of skin surrendered to sky and stone.
My half naked heart bakes itself dry,
so that even the inner chambers curl inward
like the small lobed leaves of the tall maples.

Cloistered in this canyon, lost maples
are anomalies separated from traditional groves.
In October they blush and burn, coloring the slopes,
igniting indigenous trees which sprout in their shade.

Far upstream the woman high-steps out of a deep
   pool
shouting "water moccasin!" her fast dance sending
sprays of water above her silver shoulders.

Fingers and toes grip gray rock. My tongue
darts out to wet thin lips, but my voice,
swollen in my throat, sticks, and stays silent.

Meg struggled by with the groover, looking for a place to set it. I went to help her, pointing up the hill in the thick trees.

"Is it a pain to have to be responsible for other people's stuff?" I asked.

"It's okay," she said, brushing her hair back out of her eyes. "I don't mind. Just part of the job and the trade-off is good."

"What's that?" I asked. "Working yourself to a frazzle or getting to be on the river?"

"Both. I like to work hard. The river's, well, the river is the river. What more can I say?" she said.

"Meg, I admire you so much. I hope you know how many of us wish we could do what you do on the river and how we all appreciate what you do for us," I said.

She lowered her head, said, "Thank you," and ducked into the trees.

I studied the path back to my tent so I could find the groover in the dark. Barefooted, I stepped on something sharp. Pain arced through my sole. Then, the hurt vanished, so I ignored it.

Chicken noodle soup, crackers, cheese. We stood around snacking while Robb grilled hamburgers and hot dogs and Stefan prepared potato salad and beans. Lana, Caleb, and I sat on a sandy ledge to eat and talk. When their conversation turned more personal, I moved away, found Gina, and she and I searched for sticks to roast marshmallows. Robb handed out graham crackers and pieces of chocolate bars. I burned my marshmallow black and gooey, gobbled down my s'more, then made one each for Lana and Caleb.

"Dessert is served," I said, presenting the treats with a flourish.

"Ah, you're sweet," Caleb said.

"She's too good to be true," Lana added.

I spotted Shane dumping dishwater.

"Do you want me to work on your shoulder?" I asked.

"Nah," he answered, "it doesn't hurt now."

His evening chores done, he headed down to the boats to join the rest of the crew. From our hilltop we could hear them laughing and drinking, having a good time. A group of us settled outside the ring of fire and Caleb came over and handed me a plastic jug of tequila.

"Indulge," he said. "It's good for sore throats and anything else that ails you," he said.

Nick spotted me with the tipped bottle and teased, "Laurie, I thought you didn't drink."

"I don't," I responded. "Well, not until this trip."

Everyone laughed and Caleb put his arm around me, hugging me tight.

"You loveable you," he said.

"It shouldn't be so hard," I said.

"What?" he asked.

"Love. It shouldn't be such an enigma. It shouldn't be so hard to sustain relationships, to be friends, to love everyone," I said.

"Relationships aren't that hard," he said. "Marriage is."

"Was your last one that bad?" I asked.

"It wasn't pretty," he said.

"What made it so difficult?" I asked.

"I don't know. Maybe just the boring routine of it all. The constant arguing," he answered.

"It doesn't seem to have soured you on women," I said.

"Not in the least," he said. "I rather like women."

"I can tell," I teased.

"Not to say they don't drive me insane," he countered.

"Well," I asked, "what do you do when you need an escape?"

He smiled and said, "I kayak rivers and climb mountains."

"Really?" I asked. "Which ones?"

"I've climbed McKinley and El Capitan. Done the Colorado many times, the Salmon, Desolation Canyon."

"I'm impressed," I said. "Honest, I am."

"Good. I like impressing women."

"Where's Lana?" I asked.

Caleb shrugged and said, "I don't know."

Robb joined us, offering to read from one of his books. Lana slipped into the group on the other side of the fire and I crossed over, hugged her and said, "Let's go stand by Caleb." She shook her head no and retreated back into the shadows.

"What was that all about?" he said when I rejoined him.

"She wouldn't say a thing," I said. "Just walked away. Did you two have a spat?"

"Not that I know of," he said. "After dessert she just disappeared."

Robb coughed, then said, "I'd like to read a poem by Vaughn Short called 'The Ballad of the Canyon Maid,' a tale about a muse-like spirit who lures men from the river."

I sidled closer to Caleb. He put his arm around me, so I put my arm around him and snuggled my head against his shoulder. As Robb read, his head bent close to the fire's glow, he looked up at me, making me smile. I smiled right back.

"What a perfect story," I said to Caleb. "It ties right in with mantras, being in paradise, and having good dreams."

"Your turn, Laurie," Robb said.

I tried, unsuccessfully, to recite Hopkins's "The

Windhover." The first two lines came to me, but then I drew a blank. I play-slapped at Caleb.

"This is your fault. You gave me that tequila," I said.

"I didn't make you drink it," he said, making everyone laugh.

"Damn," I said. "I practiced so hard and recited it perfectly for Hank and Gina on the boat the other day. Go on, Robb, read us another."

"Okay," he said, "how about one about a moose attack in Alaska?"

An hour slipped by with everyone sharing stories until little by little people wandered off to seek their beds. Caleb and I stayed by the fire, talking about dreams.

"Mine are violent," he confided. "Nightmares full of brutality and carnage."

"Have you ever had anyone do energy work for you?" I asked.

"No," he said. "I know what it is, though. Something like voodoo, right?"

"You goof!" I said. "It's not voodoo. It's a kind of emotional clearing. It might help shift whatever negative stuff is triggering your dreams. Do you want to try it? I'll see what I can do."

"Sure," he said, "why not?"

When the fire died down and everyone was gone, I took a small crystal that I carried in my pocket and smudged it in the smoke of the campfire.

"So," Robb said, walking up behind us, "what are you going to do, bewitch him?"

"Not exactly," I said, and turned away.

Robb stirred the last of the coals with a stick, added it to the fire, and walked out of the circle of light toward his boat.

I prepared a smooth, flat place in the sand and Caleb lay down facing the river. Moonlight brightened the setting. While warming my hands over the fire, I prayed for blessing and for healing. I knelt next to Caleb and placed my hands on his head and asked that the energy between us be that of kindness and caring, that any tension or sexual affinity ease away so that I could work solely from the power of love. I swept the air above him several times, moving off into the darkness to shake the spent energy from my hands. Lana drifted past on her way to the river, but she did not stop or speak, so I did not call out. Working slow, breathing soft and sure, I moved with hands touching palm to palm, palm to foot, palm to foot, palm to palm, and finally palm to heart.

"Where'd you learn this?" Caleb whispered.

"A massage therapist who was taking care of my dad when he was dying taught me," I said. "Here's the prayer I'm saying for you: Powers of the Universe, fill Caleb's life with good things, with light and love, with acceptance and understanding."

Caleb relaxed. I felt his tightly coiled tension ooze away. Sitting in the sand above his head, I placed my hands on his forehead.

"Goddess of good dreams," I prayed, "come to him in the night."

Caleb snored and I smiled, patted his shoulder, and said his name. When he roused, I helped him stand. We hugged by the fire, talking.

"Do you have your legs back under you now?" I asked.

"Yes," he said.

"Okay, then, good night, good dreams, and off to bed," I said, pushing him toward his sleep spot.

Alone by the fire, I relaxed, soaking up heat from the last

coals, allowing the moon's radiant light to bathe me. I walked down to the river to wash my face and listened to the night sounds before climbing the hill and snuggling into my sleeping bag.

I fell asleep right away, but sometime during the quietest hours I woke, made my way through the slumbering camp, and walked by the river again.

With an Open Hand

No matter how tight I hold the bitter truth
it escapes in the night with an uncouth coyote
who calls, and together, teeth flashing, they run,
racing far past blackness for a spoonful of stars.

So goes the game with untamed lovers I've prayed for
but lost; no hold ever stayed the day they simply
    faded away,
disappearing like dogs, leaving behind their dirty tin
    dishes
and emptiness unleashed by another morning's
    slapping sunlight.

I ask life's toughest question over and over again, but
    the answer
whispered back, is always the same: Love with an
    open hand, release
the wild geese you've sheltered and saved all summer
    into the autumn sky
to see if they can fly, grant permission for every living
    thing to live or die.

Not Far from Granite Springs Canyon

When I woke again, the moon still shone. I struggled to my feet, but could barely walk. It felt like someone was sticking an ice pick into the bottom of my right foot. I hobbled down to the kitchen where Hank prepared breakfast and Meg sliced melons and cut up oranges for the fruit bowl. Both wore headlamps so they could see.

"What's the matter with your foot?" Hank asked.

"Don't know. Something stuck me," I said.

"Hug?" he offered.

"Only if it's one of those tried-and-true famous bear hugs," I said.

Meg smiled at us.

"I just love him," I said to her and walked down to splash my face. The water lapped at the sand, the lined-up boats bobbing in the silver light.

I packed some of my stuff and when Hank yelled, "Hot coffee," I hobbled back to find Caleb at the kitchen.

"How are you?" he asked.

"Except for a nagging pain in my foot, I feel beautiful this morning, light and airy, full of love for life, calm, and rested," I answered.

"Wow," he said, reaching out to hug me with his coffee-free arm.

"And you?"

"Pleasant dreams," he said with a huge smile. "One in particular, just before I heard Hank holler. I was canoeing in slow, calm water down a stream with large trees along the banks. Naked women waved to me from the shore, beckoning me to come to them."

"Pretty cool," I said. "Perhaps it means that the right woman hasn't come along for you yet, or that you're not sure which woman you want."

Suzanne, who heard him reveal the dream, laughed and said, "I think it means that Caleb wants all the women."

"Could be true," he said, his entire face, especially his eyes, smiling.

Arm in arm we walked over for breakfast. Standing in line, waiting for Hank's banana pancakes and sausage, oatmeal, fruit and yogurt, I teased Caleb.

"It's your eyes," I said. "Your fascinating eyes. They're such an odd color. First they're blue, then they're green. They're what women call bedroom eyes."

"They aren't either," Gina cut in. "You don't even know what bedroom eyes are."

Her sharp tone knocked me off balance. "You didn't let me finish," I said.

Caleb laughed.

"His eyes aren't blue," Robb said. "They're brown, because he's full of shit."

"Good grief," I said to Caleb. "Did everybody but us get up on the wrong side of the sleeping bag this morning?"

Blue Irises

Vibrant as the river's cutthroat
a gash of red glows above the ridge
as I step out into a winter morning.

Beyond the bloody sky lies infrared,
the hot flash of all colors emerging
from a single flame of white light.

I want to see like a honeybee:
beyond the light into an inner eye
where the sky, blue irises shining,

invites me to be ignorant again
opens the day's door
on another innocent incarnation:

Eight cow elk take turns leaping a fence,
their brute beauty blending perfectly
with the sage, grass, and snow.

I finished breakfast and hobbled down to the river, rinsed the dirt and sand off the sole of my foot and took a close look. An angry red hole, surrounded by the beautiful green, yellow, and purple of a deep bruise, bloomed in the middle of my instep. I sighed: the encounter with the sharp stick last evening. Daniel saw me sitting onshore and walked over to look at my foot.

"Ouch," he said, "you better get some antibiotic cream on that. Go ask Robb. He has some."

"I hate to do that," I said. "He'll just say, 'Didn't I tell you to wear shoes?' "

"Gangrene, then," Daniel said, and patted the top of my head.

I studied the small hole. Not that serious, surely, but fear and hurt overrode pride.

Next to Robb's boat, I stood on my good foot like a crane and lifted the other one up to show the wound.

"Didn't I tell you . . ." he began.

". . . to wear shoes," I finished. "Yes, but I love bare feet and I never get to go barefoot at home. It's too cold."

While I was thinking infection, blood poisoning, amputation of the most primitive kind, I knew Robb was thinking what a sissy I was. He searched for his first aid kit, pulled out a packet of antibiotic cream and a Band-Aid, handed them to me and went back to packing gear in his boat.

I started to walk away, then stopped, swallowed a couple of times, and asked, "Robb, can I ride with you today?"

"I hoped you would," he said, his sparkling teeth gleaming through his dark beard.

I smiled back, mumbling to myself, "Why am I such a sap for attention, affection, and acceptance?"

When I climbed back up the hill to get my gear, the women gathered at Lana's tent watched as a transparent,

210

rose-colored scorpion scuttled around on her blue tarp.

"It was in my tent," she said. "When I pulled my sleeping bag outside, there it was."

"It's beautiful," I said.

"Ugh. It's scary. I probably slept with it last night," she said.

"What'll we do?" asked Helen.

"I'll go get Robb," Angie said.

"No," I said. "Robb's busy. Here, we'll just find him a new home," I said as I pushed Lana's running shoe in front of it.

"God, no," she said, when it scurried into the dark interior.

"Step one," I said. "Now step two."

I walked over to a pile of rocks, tapped the shoe upside down on the ground and the scorpion disappeared into hiding.

"Okay?" I asked, as I tried to hug her good morning.

She shrugged me off and the other women backed away, moving on to pack their things.

"You're upset with me," I said. "What's wrong?"

"Well," she said, "you asked."

She let loose with a tongue-lashing the likes of which I'd never heard before from a woman. Her brutal words, a tirade of accusations, slapped me, making me step back, covered in a cold sweat.

"Lana, God, what are you talking about?" I asked, shaking.

"You. Flirting with Caleb," she hissed.

"I was not!" I said in defense.

"You had your arm around him," she said, her face flushing.

"He put his arm around me first," I countered.

"You knew I liked him," she said, tears in her eyes.

"Of course I did," I said. "I left you alone to talk to him, I brought you both dessert."

"You always have to be the center of attention," she accused.

"I like attention," I said, feeling the heat of anger building in my voice. "Anyway, where were you? If you'd been around, Caleb would have had his arm around you."

"What if your husband were here?" she cross-examined.

"I would have had my arm around him," I said.

"What if he'd been standing in the bushes watching you behave that way?" she demanded.

"What way?" I asked, peeved.

"Like a terrible flirt," she said. "Acting like a sexpot."

"A what? That's ridiculous, Lana. Wait just a minute . . ." I said, blushing.

"You shouldn't act that way, you're a married woman," she charged.

"Who in the hell do you think you are? My mother?" I said, turning to walk away.

"If I were your mother, I'd disown you," she spat, her eyes blazing.

"That's enough!" I shouted.

"Good," she shouted back, "because I don't want to talk about it anymore."

Angie, Gina, and Helen were watching us as they took down their tents.

Hurt, confused, and more than a bit pissed off, I started toward them, but they turned the other way. They didn't want to be caught in the middle of a yowling catfight.

"You make me feel like I've done something wrong," I said to Lana, as she jammed her sleeping bag into its stuff sack.

"Lana!" I insisted.

"What?" she shrieked, whirling around to glare.

"I don't know what to do," I said. "What do you want me to do?"

"Give me some room, goddamn it. And back off of Caleb. Keep your hands to yourself," she ordered and spun back around, throwing her sleeping bag down.

"All right," I said and walked away, my stomach churning.

I thought Angie or Gina would come over to talk to me, but they stayed away, their apparent disapproval making me feel shunned. Tears welled in my eyes as I gathered my tent bag and sleep pad.

Feeling like an idiot, I couldn't figure it out. What had I done? Why was Lana so mad at me for being affectionate, for having fun? I thought we were all friends. I thought she knew that Caleb and I were just friends. But beneath all the self-examination, I seethed because Lana's blowup had burst my morning's euphoric bubble.

Walking toward the boats, I saw Caleb striking his camp. I looked back over my shoulder, but Lana was not in sight.

"Hi," I said.

"Hello there," he answered, reaching out an arm, but I stayed ten feet away.

"There's been a bit of trouble in the women's camp," I said.

"What do you mean?" he asked, lowering his arm.

"Well, it looks like they are all mad at me for hanging around with you last night," I said, my throat pulling tight around the words. "I've been branded a flirt."

"Oh, hell," Caleb said, shaking out his sleeping bag. "I'll go talk to them," he said.

"No, don't," I said. "It'll make things worse. I'll just be disgraced further by being labeled a tattletale."

He looked like a chastised ten-year-old who didn't know how to make amends.

"Don't worry about it," I said. "And I won't either, but Lana asked me to back off of you and I promised her I would. I just wanted to let you know so you wouldn't think I was snubbing you today."

"Okay," he said. "Laurie, I'm sorry. It'll be all right."

He started to say more, but I walked away. I didn't want him to see me crying.

When I climbed into Robb's boat, he was hauling the drag bag on board to put cans of soda in it for Nick and Sue.

"Need some help?" I asked.

"Nope," he said. "I am a skilled professional. I can handle the beer and soda sack on my own."

"That's self-deprecating," I laughed.

"Anything to make you smile," he said.

I wrote as we scooted along the river: "I'm not going to let Lana's tantrum ruin my day. The water's smooth and the sun's out. The light's silky, reflecting back variegated colors, rose, purple, pink, yellow, gold, green, pale blue, so I'm riding in the middle of a rainbow. Warm and content, I want to purr or hum. Sitting in the back of the boat, I watch Robb row. Sometimes he stands and pushes his whole body into the oars, sometimes he sits and just uses his shoulders and arms. He's wearing black jeans and a multicolored shirt made of soft loose material. He told me he calls it his lava shirt because he wears it whenever he's made it through Lava Falls unscathed. His pale green life vest is so faded it matches the color of the vegetation onshore as we float by. He has on dark mirrored glasses and his white straw cowboy hat is snugged down on his forehead. The oars sound rhythmic, slow, and soothing. Daniel rides in back with me. Suzanne and Nick ride in front. Suzanne is practicing her chanter. The music's both mournful and glad, mirroring the tenor of this day in the Canyon."

"Laurie," Nick said, "recite a poem for us."

"I don't have many memorized," I said. "Wait, I think I can do part of 'The Cowboy Way.' Let me see how far I can get."

Just because you ride and wrangle
Just because you wear a hat
Doesn't mean you are a cowboy
Or anything close to that.

Because cowboy's more than just a job
Or the western boots you wear
Cowboy is a spirit thing
That shows how much you care

About the land and water ways
About the horse you ride
Cowboy has a lot to do
With how you feel inside.

It's the way you treat a woman
With deference and respect
And the way you honor your country
The way she would expect.

It's the way you hold a baby
Sleeping in your arms
And the way you always try to keep
Small things away from harm.

215

It's the way you greet each morning
When the early sun comes up
And the way you savor simple things
Like coffee in a battered cup.

It's the way you treat your cattle
And the neighbor's fence you mend
It's the giving and the taking
And learning how to bend.

Cowboy is so many things
All rolled into one
But one thing that it isn't
Is a big mouth on the run.

So why don't you just rest your jaws
And listen for a change
Maybe you might just learn
Something about this range.

Hear the wind a whispering in the trees
A lost calf is calling his ma
The ouzel's singing a sweet song
Against the raven's raucous caw.

Saddle leather creaks and groans
A lone horse whickers at the gate
A coyote calls up on the ridge
To say it's gettin' late . . .

"Sorry," I said. "I've lost the thread of the poem. Can't
remember how it ends."

"Very good," Nick said, clapping.

216

"Hmmm," Robb said.

"It makes me think of my husband," I offered.

"Are you worried about him?" Suzanne asked.

"Not really," I said. "I just hope he's eating."

Everyone laughed.

"Why wouldn't he eat?" Nick asked.

"Because he just doesn't eat when I'm gone," I said. "He becomes a bachelor again and lives on crackers and milk, Coca-Colas and Snickers, white bread and potato chips."

"Sounds good to me," Daniel said.

"It annoys me," I said, "especially when I left him six loaves of homemade wheat bread, a bucketful of chocolate chip cookies, lots of fruit and salad stuff, and my own hand-crafted TV dinners."

"He's a lucky man," Robb said. "Sounds like he has the perfect woman."

"Hah," I laughed, "you might want to ask him about that."

"Parashant Canyon coming in on the right," Robb said. "Georgie White walked down it in 1946, jumped in the river with her life jacket on and swam down to Lake Mead."

A beer can floated on the edge of an eddy as we moved into calmer water.

"Look," I said, pointing it out to Robb.

"There's a beer can," he hollered to Caleb who kayaked nearby.

Caleb couldn't hear Robb, so he paddled closer.

"What?" Caleb asked.

"There's a beer can," Robb repeated and pointed.

Caleb spotted the silver can in the water and started laughing.

"I thought you said, 'There's a bear in camp,' " he said, and paddled over to retrieve it.

217

We laughed until we were sick. Caleb ferried the beer over and I stuck it into the five-gallon bucket at my feet for safekeeping.

"There's another one," Nick said to Caleb.

"Someone, somewhere, isn't going to have evening cock-tails," Robb said.

"No bear in camp?" I said, laughing.

"Such a darn shame," Daniel said.

Mid-morning we pulled into a beach.

"Short stop for a hike up this side canyon to see pictographs and stretch our legs," Robb said.

The steep trail, studded with rocks, bothered my foot. I took extra care where I stepped. A wrong move and pain shot through my instep. Wound down, quiet and attentive, the group stayed together and listened when Robb paused at different rocks to explain their history, the geology that gave them each their own unique personality. Many-colored boulders made up the dry canyon. Gray, silver, red, white, pink, beige, and some had a purplish cast as if they were in perpetual shadow.

Near an overhanging ledge, Robb crawled up an angled flat rock and perched like a colorful bird. His lava shirt, black pants, and white hat provided a striking contrast to the sandy-red walls behind him. Lana centered him in her telephoto lens and snapped a picture. She walked up next to me and said, "He is beautiful, isn't he?"

"Yes, he is," I answered, being careful what I said.

"The weather's perfect. Not too hot," she said.

"We're lucky," I said.

"We are, aren't we? Sorry about this morning," she said, and strolled away.

Inside the sheltered overhang of the ledge, pictographs

dotted the walls, images left on the rock by native peoples, a butterfly and a net, a beetle or spider type creature, a group of human forms all together, a design that looked like the letter T.

The people who first knew the Canyon spoke to me, and I bowed my head, listening, trying to make out the words. "Beware the river rocks. Beware the dark water."

Goose pimples prickled my legs and I shuddered the fear away. I made an imaginary offering, lifting my hand slightly to the sky, to the earth, to each of the four directions and whispered a prayer for the spirits who still dwelled there. "Guide me. Keep me safe."

When we walked out of the canyon, lunch waited for us in the shade of an elongated row of trees. I took my sandwich down the beach, intending to sit alone, but Hank joined me on my tiny island of shade.

"What will you do this coming winter?" I asked.

"I'm moving from Utah. I want to build myself a new house farther south. Maybe travel someplace where it's warm. Take my bike down to Baja," he said.

"It sounds like something my dad would have liked to do," I said.

"Really?" he said. "Is he gone now?"

"He died on Pearl Harbor Day almost three years ago," I said.

"Was he a good guy?" Hank asked.

"Sure," I said, "most of the time, but he had a bad temper and kept us walking on eggshells some days. Once in awhile he was a royal pain in the ass."

"Most men are," Hank said, and our laughter dispelled my somber thoughts.

"What about you? Feeding cattle, I imagine," Hank said.

"I'll help feed when I can, but mostly I'll be finishing up my master's degree," I said.

"Almost done?" Hank asked.

"Eight more months," I said.

"Hey, Hank," Shane hollered, "quit schmoozing and give us a hand here."

"See you later, sweet thing," Hank said, giving me a thumb's up sign.

My foot throbbed. All morning on the boat I'd kept it immersed in a puddle of water, reminding myself that the stabbing pain on my sole was a long way from my heart.

Finishing my lunch cookies, I took off my sandals and aqua-socks and peeled off the Band-Aid to examine the puckered hole that was smaller than the tip of a pen. Daniel came over with a little magnifying lens, Nick supplied a tweezers, and Suzanne, who had some nursing background, offered advice.

"I've attracted quite a crowd," I said.

Daniel poked and prodded the wound. Convinced there was something stuck in my foot, I squeezed the sore spot, holding my breath.

"Do we need to do surgery?" Robb asked, walking past.

"Ah," Nick said, "she's just looking for attention."

"Please, please," I laughed. "More sympathy. I'll take all the TLC I can get."

Limping toward the river to wash my hands, I searched for something to take home to John as a gift. A piece of driftwood bobbed near the sandy spit. About a foot long and two inches around, I thought it might be a branch off a cottonwood tree. Slightly curved, with an intricate knobby end, it looked oddly phallic. I waded out to get it up. Sodden with river water, it was black, smooth, and slick, small enough to fit in my pack, big enough to hold the spirit of the Canyon.

"What's up?" Robb asked, coming up behind me.

"Look," I said, feeling like I'd been caught stealing something. "I found this."

"Interesting," he said.

"Would it be okay for me to keep it?" I asked.

"Sure," he said.

"I don't want to break any rules," I said.

"What do you mean?" he asked.

"You're always telling us not to take anything from the Canyon, like rocks, artifacts, flowers," I said.

"Yep," he said. "Leave them where they are. They belong here."

"Well, we burn driftwood every night in the campfire, so I thought it might be acceptable for me to take this piece home," I said.

"It's fine," he said. "Go ahead."

"Thanks," I said, elated, and ran, gimping on my sore foot, to stash it in my pack.

"Why do you want a piece of wood?" he called after me.

"It's my gift for John," I shouted back.

We boarded the boats once again and floated downstream where the rapids were numbered by river mile: 205, 209, 217. Nick and Suzanne rode in a small, red inflatable boat called "the ducky." Before each rush of white water, Robb flagged them over and gave them instructions on how best to run the rapid. They did a great job, flying through each series of small falls like a bobbing cork, the kayakers waiting to make sure they made it all right and didn't flip.

Taking off my nylon jacket and pants, I stretched out against the pontoon side to soak up the sun, absorb the river, the blessing of the last full day in the Canyon.

Late in the afternoon, we moored the boats to hike along the edge of a wide flat rim above the river where a series of potholes were cut in the rock by centuries of the current-driven circling of stones and sand. Hot from the sun, the rocks radiated warmth. People stretched out like snakes and shed the skin of their long sleeves and long pants. Acting boyish, Robb played. He climbed down one hole and popped up in another, like the rabbit in *Alice in Wonderland*. Helen followed suit, and I joined in, being cautious about my sore foot.

Robb leapt a wide crevice and waited on the other side. I looked down. It was a long drop to the bottom. The fall from the back of a hay truck flashed in my mind. I looked across at Robb. He nodded his head and his eyes said, "You can do it." I believed him, took a big step backward, a huge step forward, and jumped. With nothing beneath me but exhilaration, I landed lightly on the other side, laughing.

"That was a leap of faith," Robb said.

"It's wonderful. For the first time in years, I feel healthy and whole," I said.

We leapt crevices and climbed through narrow holes. We tiptoed along skinny ledges high above the green water. We danced and whirled and spun, suspended between sky and river.

Light gray and oval-shaped, the egg was a low, smooth, rounded stone whose top opened into a womb-shaped space. Robb crawled inside and squirmed around, tucking his legs and folding his arms. He had a little trouble getting his wide shoulders down into the small place, but soon he curled up inside like a prehistoric bird waiting to be hatched.

"Try it," Robb said when he climbed out.

"No way," I said, "my hips are too big and I'll get stuck."

"I've seen your hips," he said, smiling. "You'll be fine."

I shook my head no and backed away.

"It would be too embarrassing if you had to pry me out of there," I said. "Let someone else try."

"Angie," Robb called. "Come here."

Angie wiggled into the egg.

"It feels warm," she said. "And safe, and comforting. I wonder if the earth made this to remind us where we came from."

We spread out along the rim and walked single file downriver to meet the boats. I followed Helen and Gina. Bobcat scat and tracks marked the sandy trail through the rocks. We climbed down through a jumble of boulders and black rock to a natural warm spring caught in the lip of the rim. Milky white with minerals, the water was murky and had a brownish orange cast to it.

"They call it 'The Pumpkin' because of its shape and color," Robb said.

"Can we go in?" I asked.

"No," he said.

"Why not?" I asked.

"Because it's sacred," he answered.

When we passed by, I bent down to touch the surface of the strange-looking water. It felt like the face of time eroding away.

I reached the beach ahead of the others and ran to the far end to find a private spot behind a boulder. The river licked at my feet while I drew a swirled design in the wet sand.

There was no understanding its dual nature. When I sank my bare feet into the sand every evening searching out the latent warmth of the sun with my toes, it seduced me. When I found it in my sleeping bag, in my clothes, in my hair, in my eyes, in my ears, it annoyed me. Every morning I shook out my sheet and sleeping bag and pillowcase and used care while stowing my sleep kit away. Yet, each evening everything was again full of sand.

Sand stuck to damp pads and the wet exterior of dry bags. Sand stuck to wet feet. Sand stuck to plates and cups and silverware. It didn't take long to get used to the fine grit that was a condiment on everything I ate. By the campfire, sand was a soft place to sit. By moonlight, sand was silver white and full of splendor. During the day the tracks on sandy beaches told me stories.

When the wind blew, the sand invaded every intimate space, even the inner chambers of my ears and the cuticles of my toes. When I washed my face with river water, fine sandy silt served as an exfoliating agent. When I tried to smooth lotion on my battered legs, sand clung to them in speckled patterns like decorations on a frosted cake.

Unconsciously, I brushed sand from another's back or butt when we rose from the beach. No matter how carefully I whisked off my feet before crawling into my tent, I woke in the morning with a quarter-cup of sand sleeping with me. Before I took down my tent each day I tipped the floor forward inch by inch, sliding all the sand toward the zippered door, then dumped it back on the ground.

I found myself loving sand, then hating sand. I cussed it when my backside rubbed red or the combination of Tevas and sand wore away the skin on my ankles, yet, I enjoyed drawing pictures in it with my toes and rubbing it between my fingers whenever I washed my hands in the river.

* * * * *

A breeze blundered up the canyon and rowing into the face of it, even with the river's downstream current, was hard work. Robb's body bunched up under the strain, each muscle gathering to give aid to the others. He stood and leaned into the oars, the pace of his movements more studied and serious than the relaxed sensual sweeping into the surface of the water just moments before. He planted his bare feet on the black bottom of the boat, his toes slightly curved for better grip. He pushed hard forward, his shoulders rotating, hands clenched, muscles contracting, then extending and releasing, before his elbows bent to pull back, his neck tightened, his hips set.

"The wind's a problem, isn't it," I said. "Where I live wind's common and most often cold, hard, and unrelenting. It roars off the fourteen-thousand-foot peaks behind the ranch like a freight train."

"Here in the Canyon," Robb said, "it is more usual in the spring, but always difficult to deal with."

"I've tried to learn to live with it, accepting its constant presence, trying not to criticize or judge it for the misery it brings to me and the livestock. Wind IS," I said.

"We have a saying here in the Canyon about wind," Robb said.

"What's that?" I asked.

"The wind doesn't blow in the Grand Canyon, it SUCKS," he said.

Then he laughed, shoving the oars forward, pulling them back, shoving forward, and pulling back. For a moment, he held both oars with one hand, set his hat a little snugger on his head, adjusted his sunglasses, and went back to rowing, the wind buffeting his body.

Lunch with the West Wind

The conversation's rather one-sided.
She talks. I listen.
She rants while I eat thin slices
of green apple with bites
of cheese and crackers.
The rabbit brush shivers.
The sage claps its tassels.
The river sighs and yawns.
She raves while I sip water
and nod in the noon sun.
When my hour is up,
I stand to go and she brushes
crumbs from my lap,
rearranges my hair,
and goes right on talking.
I walk away smiling,
leaving her to pay the check.

We entered the last few miles to our final camp and an emptiness gnawed in my gut. When I was finally allowing myself to be part of the Canyon and felt the river running in me, it was almost time to leave. Robb fished around in his mesh boatman's bag looking for a piece of paraffin to rub on his oarlocks because they were squeaking as he rowed. He pulled out a bedraggled black feather, swished it in the warm afternoon air, and handed it to me.

"Here," he said, "a gift from the Canyon. Condor feather."

"I'm honored," I said, rinsing it in the river water, then let the sun dry it as I smoothed the barbs and barbules with my fingers to reshape it.

"I'll cherish it, keep it safe, and respect the spirit of the great bird," I said.

Finding the paraffin, Robb rubbed the hard block around his right oarlock, handed me the white wax, and went back to rowing. He rowed as I held the wax in my hands, letting the sun soften it, letting it coat my dry skin.

I handed the wax back to him. He smiled at the pliable surface, rubbed it on his left oarlock, and recoated the right before sticking it back in his bag.

Gazing about, trying to absorb the Canyon's colors, I spotted a hawk or falcon soaring against a cliff face, catching the thermal updrafts coming from the river.

"Look," I said to Robb, "a raptor."

"Hmmm," he said, "redtail hawk."

I envied him the sharp vision that could identify a species so far away just by its outline against the sky.

"That's the first bird of prey I've seen on the river," I said.

I watched as the hawk hung on the face of the fine breeze, then dropped, then rose again.

"What was the poem you were trying to recite the other night at the campfire?" Robb asked.

"Hopkins's 'The Windhover,' " I said. "Should I try again?"

"Sure," he said.

Without hesitation, the poem came to me full-bodied, wings outstretched:

I caught this morning morning's minion, king-
    dom of daylight's dauphin, dapple-dawn-drawn
        Falcon, in his riding
    Of the rolling level underneath him steady air, and
        striding
High there, how he rung upon the rein of a wimpling
        wing
In his ecstasy! then off, off forth on swing,
    As a skate's heel sweeps smooth on a bow-bend: the
        hurl and gliding
    Rebuffed the big wind. My heart in hiding
Stirred for a bird,—the achieve of, the mastery of the
        thing!

Brute beauty and valour and act, oh, air, pride, plume
        here
    Buckle! And the fire that breaks from thee then, a
        billion
    Times told lovelier, more dangerous, O my
        chevalier!

No wonder of it: sheer plod makes plough
        down sillion
Shine, and blue-bleak embers, ah my dear,
    Fall, gall themselves, and gash gold-vermilion.

228

"Mmmmm," Robb said, and we were silent once more.

I looked back over my shoulder, but the redtail was out of sight.

By late afternoon only the river was talking, the pervasive quiet broken only by the dip and swish of oars as Robb rowed. I rested against a black dry bag that had absorbed the sun. Warm and at ease, I watched his shoulders sway back and forth as the boat breathed through the water. A feeling of completion flared in my solar plexus and burned there. I had been on the river a full week and the fears that followed me here had been faced down. The shadow of the confrontation with Lana and the warning I'd received, floated through my thoughts, but I brushed them away.

Robb looked aloft where a glow of last light kissed the cliffs.

"Some people say they do this because they're addicted to the adrenaline rush of running the rapids," he said. "Me, I guess I'm just a light junky."

He angled one oar and set the other and the boat responded in a slow spin that turned us in a wide full circle in the middle of the river. As he soaked up the translucent light changing the face of the Canyon, I watched his bearded face, uplifted and transfixed.

Our boat was the first to pull into the beach. The hill was steep and Robb helped us disembark after he hammered in the metal stake that would hold the boat until morning. I held his hand for a second and said, "Thank you."

I found a good flat spot to camp and put down my day pack and life jacket to mark the place as taken. As our gear was unloaded from other boats, I carried it up the hill and placed the dry sacks on a pile of large rocks.

"Thanks, Laurie," Lana said, walking up, "for finding us a nice spot."

"No trouble. I was here first," I said.

"It seems like you're always first," she sniped.

"Lana, let's not go there again," I said. "I've had an idyllic day. Don't ruin it for me."

"It's always about you, isn't it?" she said.

"Hey," I said, "you told me to back off of Caleb and I did, but then you never even talked to him all day. What's wrong with you?"

Higher up the hill, Nick and Suzanne stopped setting up their tent and watched us.

"Lower your voice," Lana said.

"Why should I lower my voice? You're the one who started this," I said.

"I didn't start it," she said. "You did. You're the one who's chasing everything in pants."

"Listen, get out of my face with this. I don't need another disagreement in my life right now," I said, stalking off.

Angie stood near the path, her eyes wide and full of tears.

"Sorry, Angie. She's just too much for me. I'm going to the river to wash," I said.

I stood knee-deep in the river and splashed myself, lathered my legs and arms and face, and rinsed over and over, but the icy water couldn't cool me down. I stomped in the shallows, anger oozing out into the sand.

"I'm so mad I can't even think," I said.

"Don't think," the river murmured. "Feel."

"This?" I said, gritting my teeth. "Feel *this?*"

"Yes. Be angry. You're hurt. It's all right to be angry."

230

"It isn't all right. All anger does is hurt someone else," I insisted.

"So what? Maybe they have it coming, if they strike first."

"Aren't we supposed to turn the other cheek?" I asked.

"How many cheeks do you have? Will you just keep taking it and taking it?"

"That's what my mother did. She used love as a shield. She survived," I justified.

"Ah, but did she thrive? Was she ever able to be who she really was?"

Furious, I picked up a stone and hurled it into the water.

I grabbed a bigger stone, slipped on the slick rocks and went down, the current grabbing my torso, dragging me into deeper water. The scream I'd started to yell stuck in my throat as my mouth gaped open. Water rushed in.

I fought the force holding me down, thrashing as I smacked into rocks, tumbling downstream. Flashing glimmers of sunlight disappeared. My limbs went limp. And then there was nothing but the distant seashell roaring of a rapid in my ears and the slow unrolling of images in the blackness.

Faded seventy-seven inside my tent. No one this far down the river. The lucky penny settling to the bottom of the pool. John saying, "Be careful." Stepping off the back of the truck. My father's unresponsive hand in mine the moment after he died. The old ones saying, "Beware of the rocks." My friend saying, "It's only water." Gina laughing and shouting, "Don't go. Come back. Come back." Helen saying, "Oh, guys, let's all hold hands." Hank lifting me off the ground, swinging me into a bear hug. Robb saying, "I guess I'm just a light junky. Close your mouth. Move toward the light."

231

I closed my mouth, felt a foot drag bottom and shoved upward toward blood-colored incandescence. Flailing, I surfaced, went down again, and under, but this time I glued my eyes on a patch of green on the riverbank. When I rose again, I clawed my way toward it, found footing, lost it, found it again and, choking and gagging, scrambled back onto the rocks.

Too terrified to cry, I crouched there gasping, taking in the sunset coloring the cliffs crimson until I regained some strength. When I could stand, I searched upstream and there sat my blue day bag and clothing within easy sight. I picked my way back through the brush and boulders, shaken, bruised and banged up, but all right.

Exposed and raw, the wind ate at my nakedness as I sat on a rock to rinse my sandy feet and slip on my Tevas.

"I've had enough," I said.

"Enough to fight back?" the river posed.

"I don't want to fight," I said. "I'm tired of fighting."

"You just fought for your life."

Aggrieved, I turned back toward my protective shell of silence.

"Don't go there," the river said. "There is nothing there. Nothing but sorrow."

I grabbed a huge gulp of air and sighed.

I studied the water slapping against the rocks.

"What do you want me to do?" I asked.

"Stand up for yourself. Be the woman you truly are. Have the courage to be who you are," the river said, her voice fading away.

I sat hunched over the water, listening, but there was nothing more, only my own soft inhaling and exhaling.

Balancing on a dry rock, I toweled off, put on clean clothes, and stowed my sundries in my bag.

As I crossed a grassy slope making my way back to camp, I met Lana, Gina, and Helen going down to the river.

When Lana split from the group and started toward me, I stood my ground, muscles tensing.

"Sheath your claws," she said, smiling. "I just want to tell you I'm sorry. I didn't mean to get so off-the-wall with you."

"It's okay," I said, turning aside. "Let's just forget about it."

"I wouldn't have gotten so upset, but you were acting like such a slut," she said.

The insult spun out of an old grave, smashing me full in the face.

"How dare you call me that!" I shouted, trying to walk past her.

"You took off your top," she yelled, "you were all over him. You weren't in your tent last night because I checked."

The black shadow of malicious jealousy flapped toward me, talons stretched, beak open, turning the moment ugly and dark.

"That's enough," I said, clamping my jaw shut on the clipped warning.

"Enough? Enough? Nothing's ever enough for you!" Lana spit at me. "Why don't you just go ahead and fuck him?"

I jerked back my hand to slap her, and she jumped sideways, stumbled over some rocks and fell hard, her knee blooming blood, her face blanched with pain.

I didn't make a move to help her. I stared down, my right fist clenched.

"God keep me from hitting you in the face," I rasped. "I don't deserve a slur like that and you know it."

233

Helen and Gina were running up from the river toward Lana, so I stomped away.

Within twenty paces my anger evaporated. Pity flooded in to take its place. For Lana, for myself, for all of us trying to find our way through life, through the dimly lit corridors of love and sexuality.

Coming down the trail, Angie found me bent over in the brush, crying.

She held me, cried with me.

"Angie, I'm miserable. What did I do wrong?" I asked. "Why did everything have to turn bad?"

"I don't know," she said. "I just don't know."

"I hate her," I said.

"Oh, Laurie, don't say hate," Angie said. "She doesn't mean to act that way."

"Why is *she* so hateful? So critical? So full of condemnation? I just wanted to be happy and carefree. To have some fun. Is that so bad?"

"No, but you moved in on Caleb and threatened her," Angie said.

"Threatened what? Her life? Her territory?" I asked, getting angry again.

Gina and Helen, supporting Lana, came walking toward us, offering hugs.

"Get away," I said. "I can't bear to have you close to me."

I pulled away from Angie and ran back to camp.

Sequestered in my tent, I rubbed my face with a dirty towel and tried to comb the tangles out of my hair. Daniel walked up and I offered him a tremulous smile.

"Foot still hurt?" he asked.

"Yes," I said, "but I don't think it is life-threatening."

"I was nominated to collect the gratuity for the crew," he said.

I dug around in my pack, found my Ziploc bag with my airline tickets and cash, and handed him a hundred and fifty dollars.

"That's generous," he said.

"Well, they worked hard to keep us fed, sheltered, and safe. Plus they entertained us," I said.

"I've been on the Colorado many times, but this has been my best trip," he said.

"Must have been our hike in the moonlight," I said, trying to infuse some playfulness into my voice.

"That might have had something to do with it," he said, smiling.

"Would you put your name and E-mail address in my book?" he asked. "I thought maybe we could stay in touch after the trip."

"Of course," I said, writing down the information. "What will you do when you get home?"

"Oh, yard work and house projects. I start teaching again in January."

"It's hard to believe it's almost over and we have to go back to our other lives," I said.

"I know," he said. "Don't you wish you could stay here forever?"

"I do," I said, "but I'm selfish. I'd only want to stay if I could have the whole Canyon to myself."

"Wouldn't that be nice? See you at supper," he said, slipping an arm across my shoulder for a hasty embrace.

I watched him stride away.

I sat cross-legged in the sun outside my tent to dry my hair.

Lana limped over, the gash on her knee crusted with dried blood and swollen.

I stiffened, held my hairbrush like a weapon, but she knelt down next to me and placed her hands on my shoulders.

"Forgive me, Laurie. I am so sorry. I think you are beautiful and talented. It's just that I'm so insecure about myself, so afraid of being rejected. I was drinking on the boat this afternoon, we were all drinking; it's no excuse, really, but I need you to know I'm sorry."

Afraid to say anything, I nodded okay. Then waved her away, doubting her kind words.

I heard Stefan call supper, but the idea of eating sickened me. Helen walked over and sat beside me, putting her arm around my shoulders.

"I know you're hurt," she said. "Lana can't help it. Your flirting with Caleb made her feel inadequate and rejected."

"Is that my fault?" I asked.

"No," Helen said, "but you could try to see her side of the story."

"Well," I sighed, "who wants to see my side."

"Listen, sweetheart," she said, "let's forgive and forget, okay?"

"I can't go down to the kitchen and face everyone. They heard us fighting. I feel so awkward and unhappy," I said.

"Laurie," Helen said, "you can't miss tonight's festivities; it will ruin the trip for you, for all of us."

"It's already ruined," I said.

"No," she countered, "it isn't, not if you don't allow it to. Come on, we'll go together."

"Helen, will you hold my hand?" I asked.

"Sure thing, baby doll," she said and reached out for me.

236

We walked into the light of the torches and filled our plates with jambalaya and salad. Sitting in the sand, we formed a circle with Daniel, Suzanne and Nick.

"Where are Angie and Gina?" I asked Helen.

"Angie's not feeling well," she said, "and Gina is taking care of her."

"Lana hasn't come down either," I said.

"Okay, let me go see if I can bring them all back," Helen said and started up the hill.

As Daniel told ridiculous jokes, I collected plates and washed dishes. A roaring fire burned in the grill and the entire group was gathering there. Below in their boats, the crew whooped it up. This was the last night of the last trip of the season for them and their voices and laughter were loud.

"Oh, no," someone shouted, "we know who you like. You like the cowgirl."

Off in the shadows near the beached kayaks I recognized Caleb's figure and walked over to hug him.

"How are you?" he asked.

"Oh, I've been better," I said, "but I'll survive."

"Everything okay in the gals' camp?" he asked.

"Not exactly," I said, "but I guess we'll get it worked out."

"Anything I can do?" he asked.

"Be good to Lana," I said. "She needs someone like you."

"I'll do the best I can," he said.

"Thank you," I said, "for your friendship. It means a lot to me."

"Come here," he said and hugged me.

Together we strolled back into the light of the fire.

Angie and Lana sat side by side. Caleb knelt down next

237

to Lana and took her hand, so I cuddled up by Gina. Helen was across the fire next to Robb. Both Hank and Stefan stood on the outer edge of the circle, their dim shapes outlined by the pale backdrop of the river. Meg and Shane leaned against one another.

Speaking for the group, Daniel made a fine thank-you speech and gave Robb our gratuity to split among the crew.

"Thank you. Our thanks to each and every one of you," Robb said. "I'm not very good at this kind of thing, but I can say that the crew and I agree that this is one of the best trips we've ever had on the river. You've been willing and helpful and a hell of a lot of fun. It's been a pleasure to know you."

We all cheered.

"Entertainment time," he said, as he stirred up the fire. "Who wants to go first?"

Suzanne read some poetry and Daniel did a hilarious imitation of Robb giving the group instructions for a day hike.

Nick performed a rousing rendition of Hank Williams singing "Lovesick Blues," "Hey, Good Lookin'," and "Long Gone Daddy." He was so good we whooped and hollered for more. So he sang "I'm So Lonesome I Could Cry."

I glanced over at Lana. She smoothed the sand in front of her knees and made a series of round patterns on that natural canvas with her flashlight. Caleb added some curlicues and swirls with his palm. Lana placed round dots inside the circles with her forefinger. Before long they created an intricate piece of art, a painting made from a hundred thousand million grains of sand.

Suzanne passed around a piece of paper and a pen that wrote in the dark.

"It's a group poem. Here's how to do it. Each of you

write one line, then pass the paper on. The next person reads only the last line written, then adds his own line beneath it."

When the pages returned to her, Nick held a flashlight so she could read our creative effort out loud. The poem was disjointed, but each image melded into another to create a memory made in words. We laughed at Stefan's line: "What to say, . . . blah, blah, blah!" And at Meg's line: "Brush first, then pee." Other lines, though, spoke of water and wind, fire and sand, people and the places we stayed. I slipped away from the circle to fill my mug with water and found Robb at the Igloo cooler.

The question left my mouth before I had time to think: "Do you want to go for a walk?"

"Sure," he said.

We moved away from the firelight, pausing to let our eyes adjust to the darker landscape. The sky shone bright with the rising moon. Robb led the way up the sandy hill, meandering around rocks and brush and trees. He did not chide me for being barefoot. We chose a spot and sat to watch the moon appear over the Canyon rim.

Far below, the campfire's dancing light outlined the revelers and we could hear laughter and the high-pitched squeals of merrymaking. Every time someone took a swig of whiskey, they blew into the bottle's narrow mouth to make a train whistle sound. The mournful wail echoed up and down the river.

"It sounds so sad," I said.

"It's always sad when a journey ends," Robb said.

"But we couldn't have a nicer night for a party," I said.

"Hmmm," Robb said. "Warm air, no breeze, a perfect moon, the singing river.

"You okay, Laurie?" Robb asked, his voice concerned.

239

When I didn't respond, he said, "I heard the rumor of trouble in the gals' camp, sensed your need to be quiet today."

"I'm okay, I guess," I said, not wanting Robb to know the sordid details.

"I saw you slip and go under this evening," he said so soft I hardly heard him.

I looked over at him.

"I was standing on my boat and saw you bathing," he said. "I should apologize for watching, but I'm not going to."

"I heard you," I said. "I heard you calling out to me, telling me what to do."

"I'm glad," he said. "I hoped you'd listen. I was too far away to do anything else."

"It was terrible and beautiful all at the same time. I wanted to just let go and let the river take me," I confessed.

"I'm glad you fought your way back," he said. "I worried for a minute that you wouldn't make it."

"You saw the fight then?" I asked.

"Yes," he said. "Saw it, but didn't hear a thing. It was like watching a silent movie."

"That's embarrassing," I said. "I'm sorry."

"Don't apologize for being what you are," he said, making me smile.

Then, we were quiet, content to savor a few moments of silent exchange.

"There's so much I want to say," I said.

"I know," he whispered.

"Do you?" I asked, wondering if he could know that the river had changed me in significant ways, that I felt like I finally knew who I was, that some long-ago wound had healed. Did he know that I wanted him to love me so badly that I hurt?

240

"Yes," he said. "I do. I understand the words you don't know how to say. No worries."

I lay back in the sand and watched the moon. I reached out for Robb and he lay down next to me and we held hands.

"What will you do over the winter when you're away from the river?" I asked.

"We purchased a piece of property and plan to build a home. I have to prepare the site and make house designs, but first, as soon as I get back to the North Rim, I need to cut some firewood."

"Are you happy there?" I asked.

"Sure," he said. "It's forty snowmobile miles off the beaten track so I never have to go to town."

We sat up and brushed the sand off each other's backs. My hands hovered near his face.

"May I?" I asked.

"Sure," he said.

And I touched his beard, amazed at how soft it was. I ran my fingers through his thick black hair and then ruffled it the same way he'd ruffled mine after the swim at Beaver Falls.

"Thanks," I said, laughing, "I've been wanting to do that for days."

He grabbed my hand and helped me to my feet, then cupped his palm against my cheek.

"Robb," I said, "get me off this mountain before I get myself in trouble."

"I wouldn't let that happen," he said, brushing the sand off my butt. "It isn't the cowboy way."

"No," I said, "it isn't."

I reached out to hug him and he held me a long time.

"Robb," I said.

"Ummmm?"

241

"I can't ride with you on your boat tomorrow," I said.

He looked at me for a moment, then nodded that he understood.

In the shimmering light cast by the waning moon we walked back down to the fire and sat together, listening to the drunken chatter around us. Lana, Helen, Angie, Gina were gone, but Stefan, Meg, Shane, Caleb, Nick and others were still up. The whiskey bottle came our way and Robb took a long pull and passed it to me. I looked at the amber liquid. Then took a big swallow. Across the fire, Nick grinned and gave me a thumbs-up.

Stefan told us stories, gesturing with his arms, pacing back and forth. The fire died down. A few at a time people drifted off for the warmth of their sleeping bags. Robb reached for the whiskey bottle, took another long swig, said, "Good night" as he squeezed my shoulder, and walked down to his boat.

I hated to give up those last minutes of companionship, so I stayed a little longer, talking with Caleb and Nick. When I finally left, I paused on the side of the hill to take one last look at the red glow of the fire, the silver-streaked river, the shadows of the boats floating near shore, and the round white face of the moon.

My Moon Shadow

At last I'm cast as the woman
I want to be: tall, thin, long-
legged, moving with fluid
grace over rough terrain.

Dipping and bending, I glide
through fences, curve over
obstacles, never stumble or
fall, finally sure of my way.

Dark and deft on a midnight stage,
I have only a small walk-on part,
but I am as aware of myself as the odd
lunar light which makes me real.

Diamond Creek to Las Vegas

When I woke in the middle of the night, I slipped down to the river and stood in the water and let it lap against my ankles. I walked back and forth on the long beach. The camp was still; no one else wandered around. I tried to go back to sleep, but sleep eluded me, so I curled on my side in my sleeping bag with my head outside my tent in the moonlight. I lay there and listened and waited for morning. By the time the sun began to gray the sky, I had packed my gear and taken down my tent. I stopped by the kitchen to see Hank.

"Bear hug?" I asked.

He swept me up into his arms and crushed me to his chest.

"Hank, can I ride with you to Diamond Creek?" I asked.

"Absolutely," he said.

"I can't believe I have to say good-bye," I said.

"You don't, darlin'," he said. "All you have to say is see you later."

Hank outdid himself for breakfast: eggs, bacon, grilled bagels, fruit, and oatmeal. I loaded my plate and sat in the sand with a group of other early risers. My bare feet and ungloved hands turned purple in the cold. Daniel, wearing fluffy down booties, said, "Here put these on."

He pulled his feet out and I slipped mine in and sighed. My toes tingled as they thawed out. When I finished my orange slices, I gave the booties back.

"Keep them," he said.

"No, that's okay, Daniel," I said. "I'll have Santa bring me a pair for Christmas."

Fingerless Gloves

Worn for years by ladies who stitched
long hours by low wood fires, waiting
for their men to return from the hunt,
from working the fields, from war,
from the warm beds of other women,
I wear them writing in the early
hours before morning, the room cold,
frost thick on the insides of windows,
the fire fighting back insistent drafts,
waiting, as I have always waited,
as I will continue to wait,
for the one I know will keep his promise
And come to me.

No one rushed this morning. As people packed their gear for the last time we stopped to chat and hug, groaning that the trip would soon be over. As I sorted through my stuff, I set aside my patterned shift and a pair of linen shorts, gift-wrapped them in a clean Ziploc bag and went in search of Meg.

"I can't accept these," she said, embarrassed.

"It's just a little gift," I said. "I have no place to wear such lightweight romantic clothes in the cold high country where I live. Besides, they belong on the river. Wear them if you want, or if they don't fit, give them to someone else."

"Thank you," she said and smiled.

"Meg, I don't want to sound silly, but thank you for your presence in the Canyon, for representing women on the river, for doing what so many of us wished we could do. Thank you for being strong-spirited, hard-working, and courageous," I said.

Then, I hugged her and that made her even more uncomfortable than my kind words.

When I turned around Robb was washing his hands at the kitchen buckets.

"That was a nice thing to do," he said.

"Just a simple gesture," I said. "I think the world of her."

"I think we boys may have fooled Meg into becoming a boatman," he said.

"Oh, I hope so," I said. "I like thinking of her here, standing in her boat rowing hard, the sunlight caught in her long blonde hair."

Robb smiled at me, dried his hands on his black jeans.

"It's been a good trip," I said.

"One of the best," he replied. "Usually I'm glad when a trip is over, but not this one, not this time."

"I wish I would have known that earlier in the week," I teased. "I would have pursued you harder."

"And I would have had to run faster," he said.

He reached out for me and I hugged him as he patted my back. We stood, brown eyes to brown eyes, looking at each other.

"Do you know," I said, "that you are just my size?"

He grinned. "Guess I won't comment on that," he said.

"Well, I'm off for the groover," he said.

"Last call for the potty," he shouted, and I laughed.

Angie, Helen, and I climbed in the front of Hank's boat and Suzanne and Nick rode in back. We hunkered down, tightened our splash gear and tried not to get wet. Few and far between, the rapids were small and not difficult. Angie drew Hank as he rowed, her sketchpad balanced on her knees. I took the last few photos on my splash camera: a shot of Hank, of Diamond Peak, of Robb's boat going into a rapid. In the shade of the Canyon walls, I shivered, anxious to be off the boat and on my way.

At Diamond Creek, trucks and buses and strangers crowded the beach, making me feel shy again and unable to speak. Confusion ruled as the boats pulled in and unloaded. I found my dry bags, pack and duffle and transferred my gear for the last time.

One of the Anasazi Expeditions' owners greeted us and presented us each with a T-shirt sporting their logo. We piled our stuff by the bus that would take us out of the Canyon, then Gina, Lana, Angie, Helen, and I trekked to the river. We each picked up a stone to wish on and threw them into the rushing water.

"Life, love, passion," I said as I tossed my stone far out into the water.

"Blessings to women everywhere," Lana said, throwing hers.

"I hope we'll travel together again someday," Gina said, skipping her stone.

"Peace of the river," Helen said, plunking her stone in an arc.

"Empty minds," Angie wished, placing her stone at the water's edge.

When we returned, Nick photographed the entire group gathered by the bus.

The crew was busy dismantling the boats and loading everything onto long flatbed trailers. I made my way through the crowd to wave at Shane and Stefan and thank Meg once more. I gave Hank one last huge long bear hug.

"I'll send you my books," I said. "I hope you'll write to me."

I hugged Caleb and wished him well.

"Silly," he said, "I'm riding on the bus with you."

"I know," I said. "I'm just taking advantage of an opportunity to get a free hug."

When I walked over to the one-ton truck where Robb was loading gear, everyone stopped and stared.

"I can't say good-bye," I said, "so I'm going to say so long."

I took his right hand, kissed his dirty palm, and placed it over his heart.

"Take care of yourself," I said. "Take care of the river for me."

A Sensualist's Apology

There is no air that others breathe
To satisfy my gasping lungs,
Or sound of air, reward of voice
To justify my seeking tongue;
The ache is not of mind or heart
The light and dark that draw apart,
It stems from some place deeper still
In blood and bone, the soul of will,
To lead me down a different trail
And on some stranger's face gone pale
Risk one finger's gentle touch
My innocent quest means that much.
So turn your eyes away, but stay,
And let me go my lonesome way
Where earth becomes my lover's arm
And sun my simple shield from harm.

Grinding up the creek bed in low gear, the bus lurched and bounced. I tried to visit with Helen, but was so tired I couldn't keep my eyes open. Angie traded seats with me so I could sit alone and sleep. The last thing I saw before I closed my eyes was Lana and Caleb sitting together, laughing.

I don't know how I slept while the bus bucked from rock to rock, but I did. I slept like a cranky, tired child who had played too long and too hard.

The bus stopped at a vehicle storage lot and there we said good-bye to Daniel, Caleb, Suzanne and Nick. Caleb and Lana were talking, so I just squeezed Caleb's shoulder. He winked at me and I got back on the bus.

We traveled on to the little town of Peach Springs on the Navajo reservation, where an air-conditioned tour bus waited to take us to Las Vegas.

Ordering sandwiches and drinks from the restaurant, we took the food with us on the bus. Angie sat next to me as we ate cheese and tomato sandwiches with Cheetos and drank apple juice.

"Gosh," she said, sighing.

"I know. Can you believe we have to leave it all behind?" I asked.

"Do you think it changed your life?" Angie asked.

"Yes. I'm not the same. I don't know what that means, but there it is. How about you?" I asked.

"I don't know, Laurie. I tried to come without expectations, but I did anyway. Everything feels all jumbled up inside me, like I'm not sure what I want anymore."

"I wonder how we'll feel about everything in a month or a year," I said.

"Hopefully that it was all worthwhile. Gina, Lana, Helen and I are already talking about taking another trip. We want to take two weeks and do the whole river. Would you come with us?" she asked.

The river beckoned, but the conflict with Lana blinked a caution light.

"Probably not, Angie," I said.

"Because of Lana," she said.

"Not only that, though the idea of going through that kind of torment again scares me to death. I hate being upset and angry. There are just too many people. It's too hectic and unsettled for me. If I come again I'd like to find a way to go to a remote place and be alone with the Canyon," I said.

"And with Robb," she said, smiling at me.

"Oh, that would be nice, wouldn't it?" I said.

"Your eyes keep closing. Go ahead and sleep. I'll be right here, reading."

"Thank you, Angie. For everything," I said.

She opened her book. Then reached over and held my hand.

Again I slept, the forward motion of the bus reminding me of the river. When I woke, we were driving over Hoover Dam. Assaulted by traffic and people, my senses tightened and slammed shut. My eyes closed as I wished the world away, but it stayed.

Knowing we didn't have much more time left together, the five of us squeezed into two seats and talked the rest of the miles away. Without even trying, Lana and I mended our fences.

The Lace of Everyday Life

Every woman's heart holds
secrets that tie into my own
until stitch by stitch
knot by knot
loop by loop
we wind threads of femininity
on the hand shuttle of the earth
decorating our different days
of silk, linen, cotton, wool
with filigreed openwork
and ornamental designs
which weave and intertwine
a netting so close
so delicate and fine
we leave a legacy of beauty
the heirloom treasured lace
of our everyday lives.

Las Vegas was not a good place to be after living on the river for nine days. Sickened by the noise, smells, traffic, the crush of people, I crouched in my seat close to tears. The bus driver pulled in at a fancy hotel on the strip to drop us off. We tangled in the aisles saying good-bye and hugging everyone one more time.

A jungle of bright lights and clanging slot machines, the hotel sported ugly flocked wallpaper and gross carpeting. Miserable, I sat on my duffle while Helen and Angie picked up their room keys. We trudged to the elevators, packing our gear, eliciting stares from those we passed.

"What's the matter with those people?" Lana said. "Haven't they ever seen women with backpacks before?"

"It's because we look scruffy in our shorts and sandals," Helen said.

"We do look rather unkempt. Like homeless girls," Gina said.

"Is anyone else as anxious for a shower as I am?" Angie asked.

Dark and stale, the room smelled like disinfectant. Helen ripped open the drapes to let in some sunlight. Angie turned on the air conditioner. Searching for semi-clean clothes, we scattered our gear across beds and tables and floor. Angie called the front desk to ask for extra towels.

"First ready, first in the shower?" I asked.

"Go for it," Angie said.

Lana perched on the sink, soaking her infected toe in hot water. The gash on her knee had scabbed over.

"That looks mean," I said. "Hope you don't lose your toenail," I said.

"Okay if I stay and soak this while you're in the shower?" she asked.

"No problem," I said.

254

The shower didn't feel as wonderful as I thought it might. The water sprayed too hard and too hot. The shampoo stung my eyes and I shaved my legs with caution, avoiding all my souvenirs.

"I can't find anything that's not dirty," Gina said, digging through her pack.

"Here, wear these," I said, handing her a pair of leggings and a long-sleeved T-shirt to wear home on the plane.

"How'd you manage that?" she asked.

"I had the biggest duffle," I said, laughing.

"Don't forget your river pants," Lana said, giving me back the pair I'd loaned her.

"Keep them. Angie said you all might go on the river again," I said. "Can I borrow your hairbrush? I can't find mine."

Scrubbed clean and dressed, we hurried down the street arm in arm to find a place to eat. With flights to catch, we had no time for the nice, quiet meal we'd talked about.

"You and Lana getting along okay?" Gina asked as we dodged people and traffic.

"I think so," I said.

"That's a relief," she said.

"God, that was a bad scene," I confessed. "I didn't know I could be so mad or feel so alone. It seemed like all of you sided with Lana against me. Was my behavior that bad?" I asked.

"Well," Gina said, "we did wonder just how many men you needed."

"All of them," I said, laughing. "All of them, of course."

One Will Never Be Enough

One will never be enough
Not one sip
one swallow
one sniff
one smile
one taste
one touch
one kiss
one friend
one lover
one day
one night
one life.

Give me
the entire apple
juicy pulp,
peel and core,
seed, stem, even leaf,
the complete chocolate cake
triple layered, thick
with tons of frosting,
the whole bitter bottle
of cheap tequila right
down to the dregs.

Give me

the full body beautiful
rough heels to wild hair,
the all and everything,
each piece and part
of the perfect picture,
total, undivided, continuous
fulfillment,
past lives
present ecstasy
infinite expectation.

We ducked into a casino and found an Italian-style cafeteria that was so noisy and crowded I wanted to hide under a table. The food looked unappetizing after our fresh-air meals on the river, but we each ordered something and Angie went across to the bar to buy beer for herself and Helen and Lana.

We hurried to eat. Animated conversation flew around me, but I was so tired I couldn't think of anything to say. I looked at the women who had been my family on the river and wanted one last photograph of us.

"Sir?" I asked the man at the next table, "would you please take our picture?"

"Sisters?" he asked as he aimed the camera.

"No," Angie said, "just girlfriends."

We leaned together, smiling, our arms around one another's shoulders, as he clicked the shutter.

Cityscape

Here where asphalt rivers run
hardened over her pale flesh
I can barely hear a heartbeat
or feel a pulse at wrist or throat.
And what happened to her limbs
is difficult to say, each one, broken,
is set in concrete and steel,
askew and unreal, and I realize
that she will never walk again.

Here nothing bends in the wind
save a few stubborn trees stuck
against curbs or confined in parks
like exotic animals, even the stones
are tame, captured in walls or cut
in slabs for statues and monuments.
I listen, but they do not speak,
at least not to me, a stranger lost
in a city where I cannot see the sun.

Here where I cannot find my way,
where I can barely breathe, I search
for her, looking around every corner,
looking into the beautiful wasted faces
of sophisticated women who shake their heads,

saying they do not know her and admit,
with sadness, that no love can be found
in these dirty, glass-shadowed streets.

Jammed with people and trash, the Las Vegas airport was miserable and messy. People sprawled on the floor because there wasn't anywhere to sit. Lana and I picked our way across the minefield, stepping over bodies, looking for a place to light. We spotted two seats next to a cowboy and ran for them.

"Hi," Lana said. "These seats taken?"

"No," the cowboy said.

"Thanks, what's your name? What do you do?" she asked.

"Mike," he said, "I'm a construction worker."

"Going or coming back?" Lana asked.

"On my way back home," he said.

"After what," Lana asked, "business or pleasure?"

"After visiting family," he said.

"What? Parents? Brothers and sisters?" Lana asked.

"Ex-wife and two kids," he said, grinning.

I listened, but did not join in. The hornet's nest buzz of so many voices not saying anything echoed in my ears. Everyone looked odd: garish clothes, coiffed hair and high heels, business suits. I closed my eyes and the river was there, running through the Canyon.

Lana held my hand as we waited at the front of the plane. The flight attendant could not find any open seats.

He led us to the back of the plane to the last row. Lana squeezed in by the window, I crushed into the middle next to a man reading a magazine in the aisle seat. Uncomfortable, I picked at the hard remnants of Super Glue still stuck around my thumbnails.

"Bless you, Hank, for keeping me together," I said.

Her shoes off, Lana leaned against the window. I curled up the best I could and we talked nonstop until the flight attendant asked us what we wanted to drink.

"I'm sorry we're babbling so much," I told the eaves-dropping magazine reader. "We've been in the Canyon."

He gave me an embarrassed glance, shrugged, and pretended to go back to his article on high-risk investing.

"Lana," I asked, "can we talk about what happened?"

"I'd rather not," she said. "I feel like such a fool."

"Well," I tried again, "can you just tell me what happened between you and Caleb? Where were you that night when he and I were goofing around by the fire?"

"In my tent," she said.

"Why?" I asked.

"I don't know," she said.

"I thought everything was fine for all of us," I said. "We ate supper together. I brought you dessert. You seemed happy," I said.

"I know," she said.

"So, what happened?" I asked.

She sighed.

"Caleb asked me about my marriage and the divorce, so I told him. I told him the truth, the good, the bad, and the exceedingly ugly," she said.

"Yes?" I prompted.

"Right in the middle of the story, he got up and walked away. He just walked away without saying anything," she said, the hurt pinching her voice down to a whisper.

She was silent for a long moment.

"The next thing I knew he had his arm around you, teasing you, and you were flirting back. You were having all the fun, getting all the attention, and I . . . ."

She stopped talking for a moment and I waited.

"You're a terrible flirt, you know," she said.

"How do you mean that?" I asked, instantly on guard.

"Terrible as in awful, as in awkward. You don't know

how to do it," she said with true humor in her voice.

"Well," I said, "I haven't had much practice. Is there a way to take lessons?"

"You don't need lessons," she said. "Seriously, what you need to do is decide if you're going to stay married or not."

"Why is this such an issue for you?" I asked. "Because of what happened in your own marriage?"

"I suppose. If you're going to be married, then you have to be married," she said, putting a big emphasis on the word "married."

"And what does that mean, being married? Does it mean you can't have friends? Can't goof around and have fun, even flirt?" I asked.

"It means you stay loyal and true, that you don't mess around with anyone else," she answered.

"Maybe that's why Caleb walked away from your story. Maybe your pain hit him too close to home," I said.

"Maybe," she said.

"Will the two of you stay in touch?" I asked.

"I hope so," she said. "He asked for my number."

"Are you glad to be going home?" she asked. "To see John? Hike with your dog?"

"Yes and no. I did miss him and I want to tell him everything that happened," I said.

"Everything?" she asked.

"Yes, everything. But I don't know if he'll want to hear it," I said.

"Why wouldn't he want to hear about it? It was a wonderful adventure," she said.

I waited a moment before responding.

"Lana, have you ever known anyone who truly deep down inside loved someone, but at the same time didn't like who they were, didn't approve of who they were?" I asked.

"Yes," she said. "Me. That's how I felt about my husband. I really did love him. I still do love him. I just don't like who he is."

"Well, I don't think John likes me very much either. I know he loves me for who I was, but I don't think he likes who I'm becoming."

Denver International boasted a rerun of the Vegas airport: a sea of lights, people, noise, and traffic. I didn't want Lana to leave me alone to get our bags while she went to find her car in the parking lot.

A young man rescued me. Taking the heavy duffles, he led me upstairs and out into the cool midnight air.

"You stay here, señora," he said. "Don't move. Your friend will come soon. I wish you a very good night."

I must have looked panicked, because he added, "Señora, it is all right. I will come back. In ten minutes, I will come again to check on you, to see if you are still here."

Huddled in the dark of the car, I stared at the dashboard to avoid seeing the expressway traffic rushing at us. Lana tuned the radio to a classical music station, but we talked all the way to her house. The confrontation on the river, if not forgotten, was forgiven.

She gave me clean towels and a hug. Then, left me alone in her small office.

The springy couch, flannel sheets, and billowing duvet were as alien to me as my sleeping bag had been ten days ago. When I undressed and lay down, I whispered Caleb's mantra over and over again just to bring the Canyon back to me.

Sometime in the middle of the night I woke and thought the furnace turning on was the roar of the river. The streetlights beamed through the windows and I closed my eyes tight, imagining that the full moon illuminated the room.

Luna

The full moon sets in the saddle of the divide,
a round rump pushing over the backside
of autumn's snow-covered cantle.

She rides the last of night down into day,
her thick thighs pushing the swells of timberline,
her bright heels pressed into stirrups of stars.

She's a silent old sister, plump
with the weight of the world hanging on her
like a crusty worn chore coat.

Oh, but look how she sits the green horse
of morning, balanced as a balloon,
her hand light on the rein of wakening.

Return to the Ranch

Just after dawn I dressed, collected my gear, and found a note from Lana on the kitchen counter: "Gone to see my kids. Don't let the cat out. Please lock the door when you leave."

I searched the house until I found the portable phone so I could call John.

"Well," he said, his voice deep and calm. "Hello there."

"I feel like a schoolgirl," I said, my voice scratchy and tight. "For eighteen years I've talked to you nearly every day. Now, in the past ten days I haven't talked to you at all. Are you okay?"

"Fine," he said. "I'm glad you're back. Are you coming the rest of the way today?"

"Yes, as soon as I can get my stuff in the car and head out," I said. "Will you be home?"

"I doubt it," he said. "The hunters got two bull elk last night. I need to take the four-wheeler up to the high country and help them pack out."

"When will you be back?" I asked.

"Before dark, I hope," he said.

"That's okay," I said, "I'll need time to unpack."

The phone was silent.

"John?" I said.

"Yes?" he said.

"I love you," I said.

"I love you, too," he said with relief in his voice.

"I'll be home soon," I said.

"Good-bye," he replied. "I've got to go. They're waiting for me."

I hung up. Then, called our daughter-in-law.

"Your voice sounds soft and sleepy and dreamy," she said.

"Uh-huh," I said. "It was a wonderful trip."

"Laurie," she asked in a motherly tone, "did you fall in love?"

"Yes," I said, "oh, yes. I fell in love with everyone and everything."

I eased down the drive so I wouldn't kick up a bunch of dust. The horses stood head to tail at the gate, swishing late-season flies. The house stood quiet, the porch door open. The cat meowed, turning circles around her food dish. Blue's absence meant John was also gone.

There was no note on the table, nothing to welcome me back. I scratched the cat's ears.

"He isn't here for me, is he?" I said in answer to her purring.

I filled the bathtub with warm water and rinsed out my splash jacket and pants, my Tevas, my pack and duffle bag. As I drained the murky water, fine gold sand stayed behind in interesting patterns: arroyos and washes, coulees and canyons, beaches and little bars. I ran my hands through that last remnant of the Canyon. Then, I rinsed the tub clean.

The soggy stick that rode with me on buses, on planes, and in cars, found a place to beach on a bookshelf. When I took it from the bottom of my backpack, it was still damp, more gray than black, and lighter as the river water evaporated from it. By evening, the stick was feather-light and dry. A tan-beige, it wore a thin coating of sand on its smooth surface. With twisted grain, it carried a trillion tiny pockmarks. I held it, my fingers curled, and turned the wood so it slid through like a screw twisting into a pilot hole. Such an erotic object, so phallic in nature, it was one of the few things in the Canyon with a masculine essence.

My cuts and scrapes had healed, but the bottom of my foot burned around a wide red circle. If I touched the spot, fiery pain shot up my leg. After a long hot bath, I couldn't stand the hurt anymore. Using the sharp tip of a safety pin, I picked away at the horny scab until I pried it off. Thin white threads of tough skin unwound, revealing a minuscule piece of green tissue with a tiny dark speck embedded on the edge. Clenching my jaw and holding my breath, I grabbed the speck with the tweezers and pulled. A drop of bright blood rushed out behind the pus.

"Didn't I tell you," I heard Robb's voice saying.

"Yes, yes," I replied, "I'll wear shoes."

Thorn

Even after so many years
some small part of him
remained embedded in me
irritating my skin, making me itch
keeping me awake at night.

I knew he was there
sharp and dark as a poison thorn;
but I was so afraid to pull him out
in case I could not stop the bleeding
in case I lost the passion, the memory,
of why I first came West.

I burned sage and sweet-grass and offered prayers of thanksgiving for my safe return. Holding the condor's feather in my left hand, I fanned the ceremonial smoke around my face and shoulders.

I saw the great bird preening its underbelly, the feather free-falling through rough air, warm updrafts rising along the canyon shale lifting it, then letting it drop again, until it settled on the water and Robb picked it up, saving it in his boatman's bag. The condor spread its wings and flew, drifting up the river and over the Canyon rim, making the circle of my journey complete.

The gift, accepted, would live on.

They say in the Canyon that what happens on the river stays on the river. But that isn't true, because I took the river with me when I left. She runs wild in the side canyons of my heart. When I close my eyes to sleep, in that sweet state somewhere between wakefulness and dreams, I hear the rushing roar of water, see her changing face illuminated by sun and moon and stars, taste her cool and silty in my mouth, and feel her wet embrace.

The river flows inside me because I washed in her water and lay on her warm sand. I allowed her access to my soul and she stayed. There are times when she comes to me calm and placid, and times when she comes to me all white water and wicked. I love her in all her phases, worship every face she cares to wear. We are separated by time and space, by mountain ranges and plateaus, by deserts and plains, but when I need her, I close my eyes, reach for her and she is there.

Sleeping with the River

Her voice calls me night after night
until finally I go down below her banks
and unroll my bed on the old bridge
that stretches between her shoulders,
to lie quiet and watch the egg-yolk orb
of the moon rise in a cloudless sky.

The jealous wind objects, complaining
through the long light hours, tearing
leaves from the withes of the willow
above my head. Nestled in down,
I am restless, wakened by recurrent
whispers of a lover I will never hold,

the never ending rush of water over
stone over stone over stone over stone.

Author's Note

Though this novel is based on journal notes taken during my raft trip on the Colorado River, *Side Canyons* must be considered a work of fiction because of the artistic license invoked to re-create events. The poems written before, during, and after the journey remain honest to the emotional experience. The only characters in this story that stay faithful to who and what they were, and always will be, are the Canyon and the river.

Laurie Wagner Buyer

Woodland Park, Colorado

May 2004

Acknowledgements

Without the following people's belief in me and my journey, I would never have found my way to the Grand Canyon. For their love, moral support, and generous gifts, I am indebted to Catherine Atkinson, Mick Buyer, Annie Chappell, Bill and Jo Murray, and Joan Wagner.

Grateful appreciation is extended to my fellow travelers on the river who provided incomparable company and valuable insight.

I offer special thanks to Matt and Susan Herrman and the folks at Moki Mac for providing me with detailed information about the Canyon.

Bless my advisors and colleagues at Goddard College who assisted as midwives when my river experience gave birth to an early draft of the story, which then grew into my MFA thesis: Margot Boyer, Alfred Corn, Lisa Grieg, Nikki Morris, David Muschell, Dawn Paul, and Jane Wohl.

Countless hugs to friends who took time to read and comment on the manuscript: Ginger Brown, Sandy Champion, Melinda Harvey, Celinda Kaelin, Kathlene Sutton, and Jan Williams.

Thanks to my editor, Russell Davis, for believing in this story and for honoring the adventure of poetry in everyday life.

Loving gratitude to W. C. Jameson for accepting and cherishing the side canyons of my heart.

About the Author

When she is not backpacking the high country, or on the road performing, speaking, and presenting writing workshops, poet Laurie Wagner Buyer lives in Woodland Park, Colorado. Her poetry books include *Red Colt Canyon* and *Glass-Eyed Paint in the Rain*. Her memoir, *Spring's Edge*, won the Beryl Markham Prize for creative nonfiction from Story Line Press. This is her first novel.